REMINISCE ROMANCE
BOOK 2

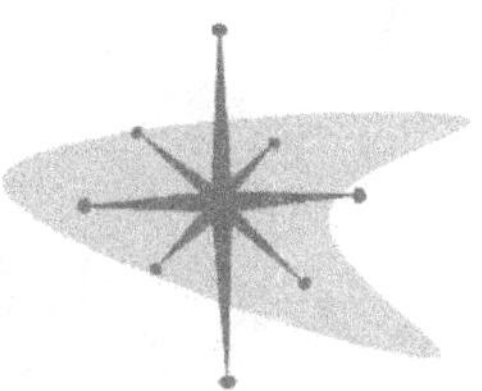

Reminisce line of books by Kirk House Publishers

For Mom

My beautiful mother, Mary

REMINISCE ROMANCE
BOOK 2

A Collection of Stories by Kirk House Publishers

First Edition
Paperback ISBN: 978-1-952976-83-4
eBook ISBN: 978-1-952976-84-1
Hardcover ISBN: 978-1-952976-85-8

Library of Congress Control Number: 2022943887

Cover and Interior Design by Ann Aubitz
Images on cover from Bookbrush
Illustrations painted or designed by Ann Aubitz
Images from AdobeStock

Published by Kirk House Publishers
1250 E 115th Street
Burnsville, MN 55337
Kirkhousepublishers.com
612-781-2815

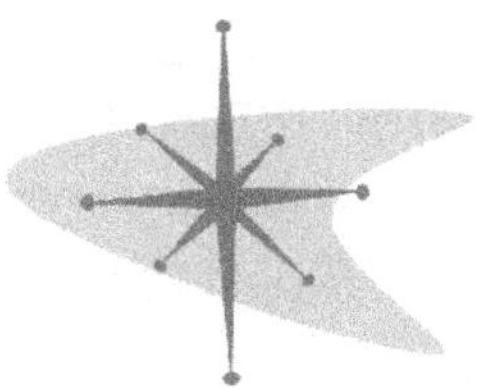

FOREWORD

When Ann Aubitz from Kirk House Publishers called me about the new line of books she was publishing for older readers, my ears perked up. I knew this was an underserved market. Ann explained her series would be different from the books currently available. Her books were actually inspired by an elder, her 96-year-old mother, who still enjoys reading.

I was excited to review the books myself, as so often, books for our elders have small print, they are hard to hold, or they have storylines that are too complicated to comprehend, or on the other side, they are overly simplified and childlike.

What I found was Ann's books (the Reminisce book line) were designed to be dignified and intriguing. In addition, they would meet multiple needs:

1. Large print for older eyes.
2. The larger-sized book makes it easier to hold, as it is common for fine motor skills to decline as we age.
3. Intriguing storylines for all ages. This allows flexibility to share intergenerationally, allowing grandma or grandpa to read to their grandchildren, or their grandkids can read the book to their grandparents, if they are in the mood to share.
4. Along the lines of intergenerational, the books also can teach children a bit about the past and to engage in conversation about the good old days that elders refer to.

5. These books are ideal for a wide range of people and abilities of various ages, and for those with early cognition issues, they are *ideal*!

The stories are set in the 1940s, 1950s, and 1960s in an easy-to-read, short-story format in the genres we love: mystery, romance, ghost stories, and science fiction. Large type and full-colored illustrations make the stories accessible to all readers, many of whom may have their own special memories of those periods of history.

This series will meet a wide range of needs, enabling many people who love to read to continue having that pleasure.

I highly recommend the Reminisce book line for your special someone that still loves to read.

~Lori La Bey, founder of Alzheimer's Speaks

Alzheimer's Speaks is a Minnesota-based advocacy group and media outlet making an international impact. Our goal is to shift dementia care from crisis to comfort by giving voice to all and raising those voices to enrich lives by sharing critical information, personal stories, resources, products, and tools from people and organizations at all levels around the world.

Website: https://alzheimersspeaks.com

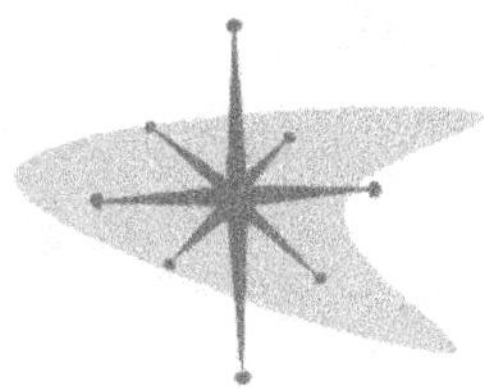

TABLE OF CONTENTS

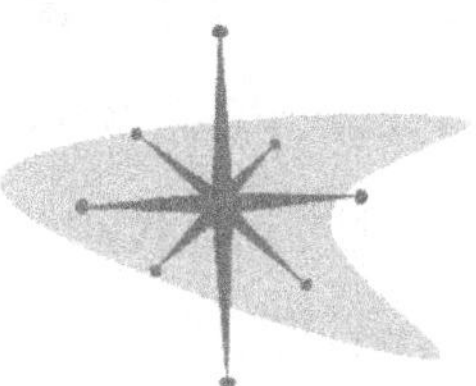

INTRODUCTION

When I was young, the greatest joy for me was reading books. But, of course, this was before reading was cool like it is now. It was a time when my friends were playing their first computer games, but not me—my nose was always buried in a book. In those stories, I went to far-off places and had amazing adventures. In those stories, I could be free.

I credit my love of reading to my mom. Born in 1926 to a family with sixteen children, she never finished high school, but she had a thirst for knowledge and reading that thrived throughout the years.

I remember only a few times while growing up that my mom didn't have a book, magazine, or word puzzle in her hands—she had an insatiable quest for knowledge.

In her senior living facility library, she discovered a book that she loved. It was *Little Women*, by American novelist

Louisa May Alcott. It was altered from the original book in a good way. This book contained illustrations and larger print. My mom would run her fingers over the pictures to remember a time long past. She read and reread the book.

Unfortunately for her, there were no other books like this in the library. She tried and failed to read books with more complex storylines and smaller type. She would get frustrated and distraught because reading no longer brought her joy.

This is why I started this line of books. It is for people like me and my mom that *love* to read. These books are meant to be easy to read, have a complete storyline, and help readers remember a time long past and *to reminisce.*

Kirk House Publishers is proud to present the Reminisce Line of reader-friendly books. Written by several authors, the stories are set in the 1940s, 1950s, and 1960s in an easy-to-read, short-story format. Large type and full-colored illustrations make the stories accessible to all readers, many of whom may have their own special memories of those periods of history.

Happy Reading!

~*Ann Aubitz*

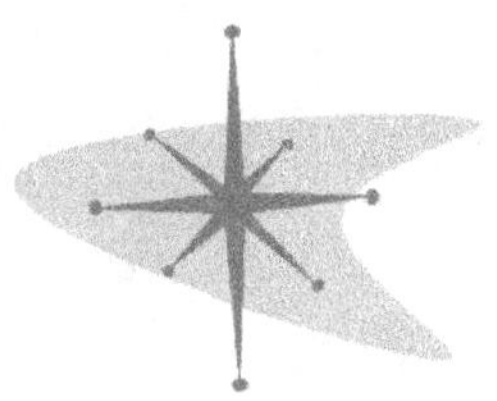

DARE TO FIND LOVE
By Lynn Garthwaite

Linda bent down to pick up three-year-old Robin and carried her through the revolving door at the entrance to Southwood Mall. The squirming little girl insisted on being set down on the other side. "I can walk by myself, Mommy."

"I know you can, sweetheart, but those revolving doors can be tricky for a little one."

"I'm not little," Robin insisted. "I'm three." She held up three fingers to make the point.

Linda smiled at her daughter, getting so big, so fast.

The two of them made a couple of quick stops for a few of the items on Linda's shopping list, and then Robin spotted the bookstore.

"There it is, mommy! Books! Let's get some books!"

Linda smiled at her daughter's enthusiasm for something the two of them always shared delight in. Books were their favorite getaway—their door to fun worlds with fantastical creatures and adventures around the globe. This was always their favorite stop when they came to the mall.

Once inside, Robin raced to the row of giant stuffed beasts that lined the area near the children's section. A four-foot-tall unicorn was Robin's favorite, but this time she seemed drawn to the six-foot giraffe next to it.

Linda's eyes were drawn to the man behind the counter. He had been working at this bookstore for quite some time, and Linda couldn't help stealing some glances at him every time they were in the store, watching his easy way with customers and enjoying that smile that lit up the store. She knew his name was Paul, but only because of his nametag. She'd been too shy to strike up a conversation other than the quick words when she brought books to the counter to buy.

Her attention was interrupted by a loud thump and a cry from Robin. Linda turned to see that Robin had tipped over a metal stand, and books were strewn across the floor. Robin was rooted to the spot, both startled and fearful that she had done something wrong.

Linda got to the pile of books about the same time that Paul did, and both were quick to allay Robin's tears that ran down her cheeks.

"Don't worry about it, honey," Paul told her gently. "Just look at how easy these are to pick up."

Linda used a tissue to dab at Robin's tears. "It's just a big 'oops,' sweetie. Let's help pick them up."

Robin recovered quickly from her fear and started picking up books and handing them to Paul, who returned them to the metal stand that he had stood back up into place.

"Here you go, book man," said Robin for each book she picked up. Pretty soon, Linda and Paul giggled at Robin's enthusiasm for picking up and handing off books.

"You can call me Paul if you want. What's your name?"

Robin did a little spin around to add flair to her answer. "Robin Elizabeth Peters. And I'm three."

Paul laughed. "Well, I'm Paul David Keaton, and I'm at least twice your age." He turned to Linda, smiling that smile she had been admiring from a distance.

"How about you? Care to share your personal data?"

Linda looked down shyly but couldn't help but grin.

"Linda Marie Peters, and I'm raising an imp instead of a human being."

Paul laughed and finished refilling the metal stand with the books.

"I've seen you two here before. If I remember correctly, you bought *Twig* the last time. One of my favorite books of a little girl who builds her own fantasy world in her backyard."

"You've read it? We just finished it, reading a chapter a night. Robin now has plans to build a little house in our backyard for her own fairy."

Paul placed a hand over his chest and turned to Robin. "A girl after my own heart. Let's see if we can find something else today that will be just as full of fairies and adventure as *Twig*."

Linda watched as Paul pulled some books on a shelf to show Robin. She was captivated by his gentle nature and couldn't help but find herself attracted to his handsome face. *But stop*, she reminded herself. *You're a widow, and Will has only been gone three years. Get a hold of yourself.*

Feeling guilty for the attraction she felt for another man, she quickly helped Robin make a selection of one picture book and one early chapter book and paid for their purchase. As they walked to the store's exit, Robin turned to wave at Paul, who smiled and waved back.

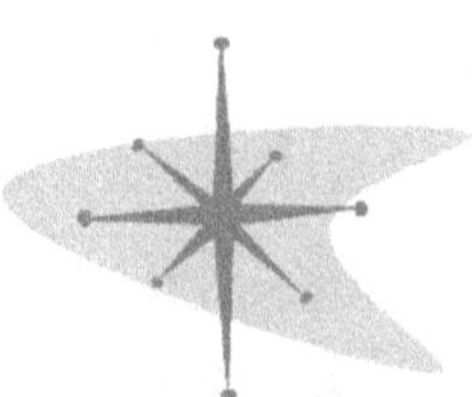

Later that day, Linda and Robin left their tiny little bungalow home and walked two blocks to the neighborhood ice cream parlor. Dinner had barely settled in their stomach when both agreed that an ice cream cone would be the perfect end to a fun day.

Once inside, Linda focused on the ice cream in the tubs, open in the cooler to display the flavors available that day. Robin let go of her hand and ran to a table in the corner, calling back to her mom, "Look, mommy, it's the book man!"

Sure enough, Paul was sitting at a table in the corner, a book in his hands and a small dish of ice cream in front of him. Surprised at the attention, he looked up and smiled as he saw the delighted Robin running toward him. Linda was a few steps behind her.

"I'm so sorry. Robin can get a little stranger-friendly sometimes."

"Don't worry about it. And besides, we're not strangers. We both inhabit the world of fairies, unicorns, and friendly lions...at least in our dreams."

Linda smiled. "Very true. I used to live in that same world as a young girl, so I know where she inherited that."

"There is never a reason to leave that world. Until, of course, the real world needs you now and then." Paul gave her a wink.

Linda guided Robin back to the counter, where they both chose their favorite flavors. When they turned to find a seat, the only openings were where Paul sat. He gestured a welcome to them, so they joined him, and together the three ate their ice cream and talked about books and the best way to have fun.

After a while, Robin went to the back of the ice cream parlor, where several other children were playing a game of pretend hopscotch. Keeping an eye on her daughter, Robin relaxed a bit and enjoyed the conversation with Paul.

"How did you end up working at the bookstore?"

Paul looked up at the ceiling, thinking back. "I got a job right out of college working at an insurance company, but never really felt like that was my calling. My brother Gary and I, both avid readers and crazy people, started plotting our course to own our own bookstore. He went off to fight in Korea, but I couldn't join him because I had broken my shoulder as a teen, and it never healed completely. I don't have complete flex of that shoulder to this day, although I keep working at it."

"So you took a job at the mall bookstore in the meantime?"

"Yes, it was with the plan that I'd learn all the ins and outs so that we'd be ready to go through with the plan when he came home. The problem was that Gary never came home. He died in Korea."

Linda touched his arm with sympathy. "I know what you are feeling. My husband died in Korea too. Two months before Robin was born."

Paul's eyes clouded with sadness. "I'm so, so sorry. You must have been devastated. And Robin, never knowing her father...."

"It's been three years, and I still can't figure out exactly how to move ahead with my life. I'm sure you feel that way too."

"It's true, although in a different way. I can't picture starting up that bookstore without Gary, so I'm staying the course until I figure out how to do that."

"I think most people who experience a sudden death of a loved one," said Linda, "go through a period of time where they not only feel the horrible loss but lose the ability to put one foot in front of the other with regard to the rest of their lives. In a way, Robin's birth forced me to face everything in front of me. She needed me to be whole, and with the help of my family, I think she has done very well."

"But what about you? What are your dreams? What do you want?" Paul leaned into Linda, interested in her answer.

"I think I've managed to set that aside. The picture I had of the white picket fence, the husband and the child, or children...none of that has turned out the way I thought it would. And I don't often say it out loud, but I would love to work in a private investigator's office. Maybe help with research and writing reports."

"Maybe it's time for both of us to get brave again. Dare ourselves to refresh those old dreams and make them happen. May I take you out to dinner sometime?"

Linda was surprised by the invitation, and her first reaction was to refuse. "No, I couldn't. It...I can't."

Paul was gentle but pushed just a little bit. "Try it, Linda. Try to push that boundary you imposed. It's just dinner. I'd love to see you again."

Linda paused and looked over at Robin, who was laughing and being silly with her new friends.

"I suppose I could do that. Just dinner."

"Just dinner. I would love that."

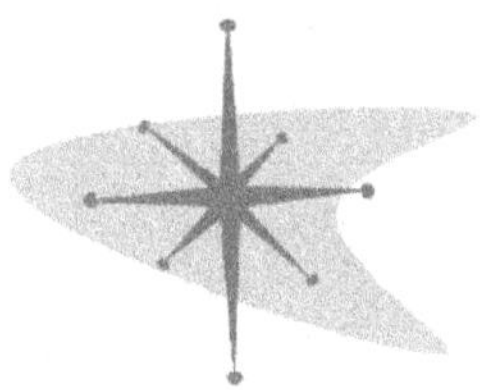

Two days later, after an evening that Linda was surprised she enjoyed as much as she did, Paul walked her to her door.

"Tell your parents I appreciate their babysitting Robin so I could have an evening with you," said Paul.

"They've always been so much help for me. I think I would have lost my mind if they hadn't been here, especially when the terrible twos hit."

Paul laughed and then leaned in cautiously, trying to read Linda's reaction. "Thank you for daring to have dinner with me," he smiled and then very gently kissed her on the lips before turning to leave.

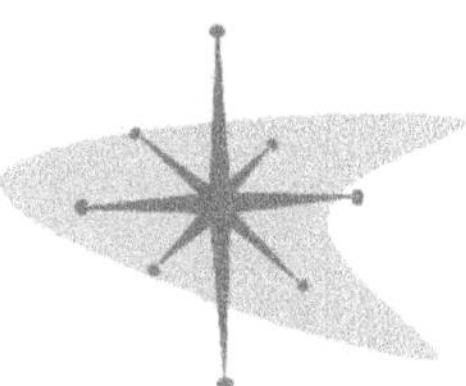

Paul called again two days later, and pretty soon, Linda was finding herself willing to put more steps in front of the other with regard to exploring the new relationship. She still felt a pang of guilt, as if she were being unfaithful to Will, but she talked to his spirit in her quiet moments and felt calm that he would want her to find happiness. She finally felt ready to break another barrier and invited Paul into her home to sit at the same table where Will had once sat.

Paul arrived on time with flowers in one hand and a small package for Robin in the other. Robin was the one to open the door for him, and she squealed with delight when she saw him.

"Mommy, it's the book man again. Can he stay for dinner?"

Linda was right behind her and laughed. "Yes, he most certainly can stay for dinner. That was actually the plan."

Paul handed the bouquet of flowers to Linda and then knelt down to hand the package to Robin. "This is for you, Robin.

You're the sweetest three-year-old in the whole world, so I thought you should have this.

"What is it?" Robin held it with awe.

"Open it up and see," said Paul.

Robin tore the paper off the package and shrieked with delight at the stuffed unicorn she held in her hands. She immediately hugged it tightly. "I love it. My uni, my uni."

When Robin ran off to play with her new toy, Linda snuck a quick kiss with Paul. "Thank you for the flowers. Come on in the kitchen. Dinner is almost ready."

As they passed by the fireplace, Paul's eyes caught a small framed medal with colors that he recognized.

"Linda, was this Will's medal? From Korea?"

"Yes, I received it in a package about a month after he died."

Paul appeared shaken.

"I recognize that symbol and those colors. The second Infantry Division, right? Nickname Indianhead. Their motto was 'Second to None.'"

Linda looked at him, confused. "Yes, how did you know that?"

"Because that's where Gary served too. Stationed at Camp Humphreys in South Korea. Linda, what date was your husband killed?"

The air became quiet, both of them sensing something like electricity passing between them.

"He died in the Battle of Heartbreak Ridge on October fifth, nineteen fifty-one."

Paul lowered his chin to his chest, taking this all in. He finally spoke, a little catch in his voice.

"Will and Gary served together. And died together. That's the same place and date where Gary was killed too."

Linda's hand went to her mouth, startled. Both of them were quiet for a moment. Finally, Linda managed a question.

"Do you believe in coincidences? Or do you think there is some higher power guiding us to places we need to be?"

Paul looked her in the eyes. "I've always believed in a higher power, but I had never thought about whether our own loved ones have some influence on the other side. But now I'm wondering if Will and Gary have made sure that we found each other."

Linda moved in to put her arms around Paul, who wrapped his around her too.

"I think it's possible that somewhere out there," Linda whispered, "two souls have conspired together to push us to get back into life and work toward our dreams."

She tilted her head back to look into Paul's eyes.

"And I'm grateful they did."

Paul smiled and leaned in to kiss the new love of his life.

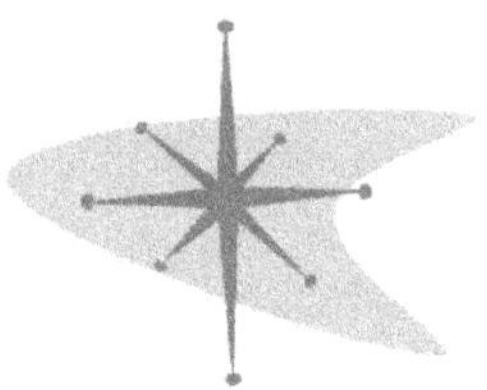

About the Author

Lynn Garthwaite is the author of eleven books, including the Dirkle Smat adventure book series, three picture books for clients (Radio Flyer and Shutterfly), and a historic nonfiction for all ages titled *Our States Have Crazy Shapes: Panhandles, Bootheels, Knobs and Points*. She has also written a mystery/thriller, *Starless Midnight,* and an updated nursery rhyme book titled *Childhood Rhymes for Modern Times.* In 2022, *Your Children Can be Writers: 40 Story Prompts to Spark their Creative Genius* was released. Lynn is also a copyeditor for three magazines, a publisher, and a member of Sisters in Crime.

ICE CREAM SHOP

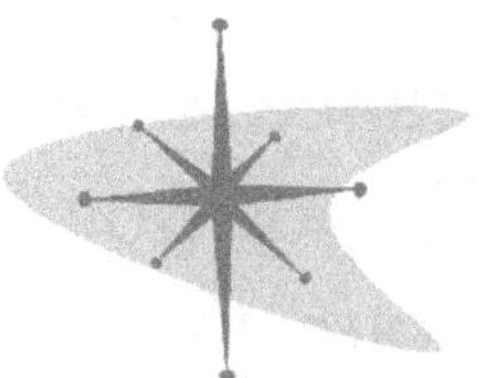

THE GREEK DREAM

By Ava Florian Johns

The minute Kat stepped out of the car onto the crunchy white gravel path, she knew leaving her incredibly dull life behind in America was the right move. Kat took a deep breath and inhaled the salty ocean air. The morning sun was high in the sky, so she put her hand above her eyes to take in the fantastic scenery.

The impatient driver made a sweeping gesture with his arm. "You'll see the villa as soon as you walk around that curve," he said as he hastily unloaded her luggage from the trunk and took off in his taxi, spraying white rocks all over her bags. *So typical,* she thought, but nothing could get her down. She was glad she left behind her dull existence in New York for the glorious Greek islands and a fresh start.

A month ago, she had intended to marry Alfred Anderson, a boring accountant type, who broke off the engagement while she was standing at the altar, citing cold feet. Later she learned it wasn't cold feet that Alfred had but another woman with a baby on the way. And that was the end of their boring romance. Well, good riddance Alfred.

Leaving her secretarial position at Alfred's company, she signed on with a Greek tour company specializing in island-hopping tours. She didn't know much about Greece except for what her Greek grandmother told her—Kat suspected her grandmother's stories were based more on fiction than fact. Nonetheless, she packed up and made the trip across the ocean. She had spoken with the owner of the villa and tour company, and he was excited that she was from the United States and could speak English to their many American visitors.

She wound her way around the gravel path and found an open doorway to the check-in desk. The owner indicated that she would be living and working at these villas. She was hired as a tour guide but could also help at the hotel during her off-hours if needed.

Once inside the lobby, she let her gaze sweep the room. It was a lovely, airy space, with doors opening onto a sunny terrace where people enjoyed breakfast. In the distance, she caught her first glimpse of the incredibly blue Aegean Sea.

Kat walked up to the desk where a beautiful Greek woman was standing.

"Good morning. I am Katerina Pappas, the new tour guide."

"Ah yes, Miss Pappas, it is good to meet you. My name is Sofia Vlachos. We have been expecting you." She had a thick Greek accent, so Kat listened to her intently. She guessed that Sophia was around fifty years old. She had long dark hair, little tufts of gray that stuck out from her temples, and an open, friendly face.

The woman grabbed her hand and gave Kat a friendly, firm handshake.

"It's good to meet you as well. I am excited to be here." Kat liked her instantly and gave her a hand an extra pat.

"We're happy to have you. Mr. Papadopoulos has been thrilled about your arrival and the expansion of his tour business. I think the villas keep us too busy, but there is no telling him that."

Kat wasn't sure what to say, so she smiled and said nothing. Suddenly a tall, dark-haired, olive-skinned, exceedingly handsome man appeared behind the check-in counter and stood behind Sophia. She imagined the Greek gods of the past looking like the man before her.

"Oh, my beautiful Sofia, what are you telling our new employee? You know, I want to offer our guests a full experience of the islands we love." He then turned his attention to Kat. "And you, my dear, must be Miss Pappas." He came around from behind the counter and kissed Katerina on both cheeks. She was surprised at first but realized this was a customary greeting for people in Greece. She needed to get over her American sensibilities.

"Yes, I am Katerina Pappas, but you can call me Kat."

"I like it—Kat, very American. Welcome to the Villa Papadopoulos. I am Nickolas Papadopoulos. My great-grandfather built the villas over one hundred years ago, and they have been passed down in our family and finally to me." His accent was less pronounced than Sophia's, Kat thought. Then she remembered from their conversation that he mentioned studying at Oxford University in England.

"Well, thank you for giving me this opportunity with your company. I am very grateful and excited to get started." Kat was finding breathing difficult with her handsome boss smiling at her.

"I will have Sophia show you to your room, and then we will start our training tomorrow morning. How does that sound?"

"It sounds wonderful. Thank you, Mr. Papadopoulos."

"You are very welcome, Kat."

Nickolas knew the moment he met Kat that he was in trouble. He had no idea how he would refrain from telling her how beautiful she was or kissing her plump red lips. She had long dark hair that cascaded over her shoulders and flawless olive skin that she no doubt inherited from her Greek grandmother. They had spoken on the phone to see if she was suited for his new tour guide position, but her voice didn't give him a clue of what she was like in person. On their call, she told him her grandmother's tales about the Greek islands' magical love-inducing powers. Of course, he had heard these all before, but still, he imagined the two of them falling in love on the islands when she told him the stories. From the phone calls, he had a fantasy version of Katerina in his head, but nothing compared to the luscious woman in front of him. He had never felt that way about a woman he had only spoken with on the phone, but now that he had met her, he knew that that could be a real possibility. He shook his head as he walked down the hallway away from the temptress.

When Nikolas came out behind the check-in desk, Kat knew she was in for it. Now *he* was the man of her dreams. When she envisioned the man she would spend her life with, she never imagined she would be with someone like her ex-finance, Alfred. He was a sniveling little waif of a man. He was a couple of inches shorter than her and started wearing lifts in his shoes to be as tall as her. He also forbade her to wear heels when they were out in public. She slapped her head with her hand. She shouldn't be wasting her time thinking about him. He was thousands of miles away, and she was starting a new fantastic adventure.

"Miss Pappas, please follow me." Kat hoped Sophia hadn't had to say it to her more than once. Daydreaming about her new boss wasn't an acceptable practice in any country.

"Thank you, miss Vlachos. Is it Miss or Mrs.?" Kat asked, taking position behind Sophia on their walk through the villa grounds.

"It is Miss, but you can call me Sophia."

"Thank you, Sophia, and you can call me Kat."

"Kat, you don't go by your Greek name Katerina?"

"No, not usually. In America, Kat was easier, shorter, I guess. Maybe I should go with Katerina now." Kat was happy to be getting the chance to speak with another woman. Alfred didn't like her girlfriends and preferred that she not spend any time with them, so Kat wasn't close to anyone anymore.

"If you don't mind me asking, Katerina, what brings you to the islands? It is odd for a single woman to pick up roots in one country and take a job thousands of miles away in another country where she has never been." Sophia cringed and realized that she may have been a little too frank. "Sorry if that is too blunt of a question—I was just curious."

"It is not too blunt at all. It is nice to talk to someone about it. About a month ago, I was engaged to be married to my boss. My groom left me at the altar and had his brother give me a note that said he had cold feet and couldn't marry me." Katerina stopped walking. As soon as she did, Sophia stopped too. Kat took a deep breath and continued. "I later learned from his best friend that Alfred had been cheating on me. He didn't have cold feet; he had gotten another woman pregnant."

Sophia gasped. "Oh, my goodness, what did you do?"

"I ran out of the church and never looked back. I should have known better than to get engaged to my boss. So, I quit my job working for Alfred's accounting company and hightailed it to Greece."

"Why Greece?"

"My grandmother was Greek, and she was the only family I ever had. My parents died when I was a baby, so my grandmother raised me as her own child. She loved Greece and wanted to come back someday, but she died from cancer two years ago." Kat sniffed and realized that tears were streaming down her face. "I am so sorry; I know you didn't expect me to go blabbing my entire sob story."

Sophia grabbed Kat and held her in a soft embrace. "Oh, my dear, you have been through so much. You go ahead and cry." Kat sniffed again, and Sophia pulled out an embroidered handkerchief for her to wipe her eyes.

"Thank you for being so kind. I haven't had anyone to talk to, and it feels good to get it off my chest."

"You are welcome, my dear Katerina, and I look forward to working with you."

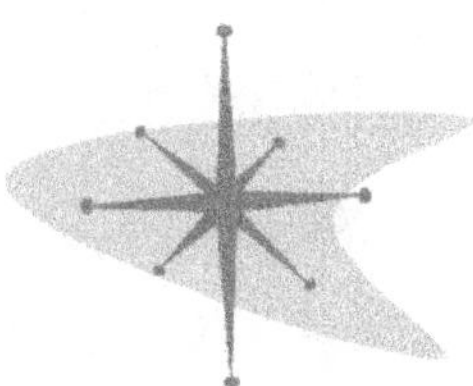

Sophia led Kat to her villa without any more tears. The room was small but well-kept. It held a twin-sized bed with a blue quilt the color of the summer sky, a small desk, and a large picture window that looked out over the Aegean Sea.

"It is perfect!"

"I am so glad you like it. We are very proud of our little villas."

"I can see why—it's beautiful." Kat spun around the room, taking in all the ambiance.

Sophia smiled knowingly, then spoke, "We have a staff dinner at eight tonight. Please join us where you checked in, in the main lobby."

"I will be there. Thank you, Sophia."

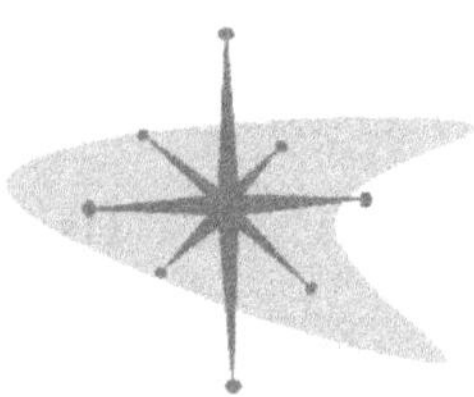

Kat walked out of her villa, excited to start her adventure. She heard through her new gorgeous boss that the food served in their restaurant was the best on the island. Of course, he was biased, but she was still excited about tasting authentic Greek cuisine. As she walked the gravel path back to the area, she was suddenly captivated by two large white birds flying out of the trees in wide circles. She had no idea what species they were, but excitement moved through her. The birds made her think of the signs of fate her grandmother told her throughout the years.

"Ah, Katerina, I am so glad you found your way back to us." Nickolas gently guided her with his hand on the small of her back to the dining area. "Let us join the others for a grand celebration."

"What are we celebrating, Mr. Papadopoulos?" Kat hesitatingly asked. She hoped that she wasn't daydreaming when Sophia had mentioned it.

"Your arrival, of course." When he saw the surprise on her face, he added, "And the expansion of my sightseeing business."

They were silent as they walked through the cobblestone lobby and entered the open atrium-style dining room. There, in the middle of the room, sat more than twenty people all waiting for them.

"Everyone, I want you to meet Katerina Pappas, our new tour guide. As you know, from the mid-nineteen fifties until now in nineteen sixty-three, Greece became a destination for a new brand of traveler known as the 'tourist.' Because of the tourists, we are expanding our business and offering our guests a full experience. They will be able to visit this island and many others. It is the ultimate Greek island experience, exploring Mykonos, Paros, Santorini, and Ios. We will call it *island hopping.*" The employees cheered this announcement as Nickolas dramatically swept his arm toward Kat in a grand gesture. He introduced them to Kat individually and then gave her a moment to speak.

"Thank you all for the warm welcome. I look forward to working with you." Kat cleared the lump in her throat as she spoke.

Throughout the meal, Nickolas couldn't take his eyes off Kat. So much so that Sophia noticed and gave him a warning with her eyes.

He sighed. "What, Sophia?"

"I see you looking at our new employee with lust in your eyes." Sophia looked at him with a disapproving glare.

"You are imaging it." Nickolas laughed and turned away from her discerning eyes.

"No, I am not. Remember, I have seen you in love before. You can't fool me, and you can't mess with her. Her no-good fiancé just stood her up. She is not ready for love."

"No one is ever ready for love, my dear Sophia. First, it hits you like a ton of bricks, then you hang on and enjoy the ride."

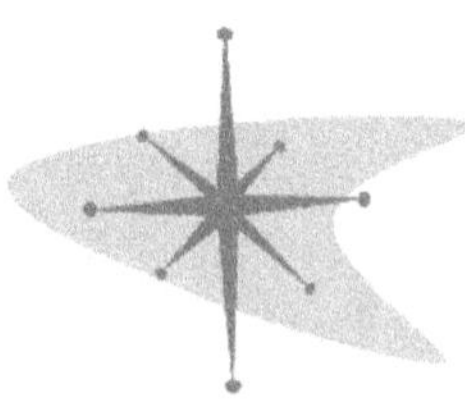

The following day, Kat and Nickolas met in the check-in area at nine for her first training day. Unfortunately, she had stayed up too late the night before and was a bit groggy. She needed to keep her wits about her if she was going to keep it strictly business with her new boss.

"Good morning Katerina. How are you feeling this morning?"

"I am doing well. Thank you, Mr. Papadopoulos."

"Mr. Papadopoulos sounds much too stuffy. Please call me Nickolas."

"But I noticed last night that everyone else calls you Mr. Papadopoulos. So I think it would be best that I don't sound too familiar."

"When it is just the two of us, Nickolas would be fine."

Kat didn't say anything after his remark, so he let it go and figured he would try and focus on business.

"Today, we are going to go to Santorini. We will take the ferry and experience the wonders that the island has to offer. My goal is to provide our guests plenty of time to explore charming villages, local shops, volcanoes, natural coves, and sun-soaked beaches, with plenty of time for sunbathing, swimming, and nightlife as well as a bit of ancient history in between. So I want you to travel and experience the sites for yourself, as well as study the books we have on the culture of the Greek islands. What do you think?"

"I think this job sounds too good to be true."

They shared a fiery look between them, then Kat looked away, and the moment was gone.

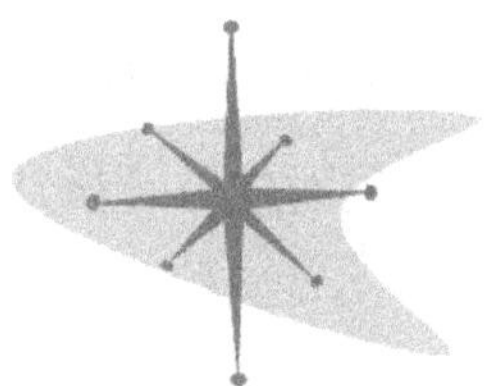

A month later...

Kat was enjoying her job immensely. She would give tours all day and sometimes into the night for those guests that enjoyed the nightlife. She also worked at the villas, checking people in when Sophia needed additional help. Her life was perfect, except for the nagging attraction to Nickolas. She didn't want to get involved with him for fear that it would turn out the same way as it did with her and Alfred. This was the one place where she felt she truly belonged. She loved the culture, the people, and everything about the islands. But she had to admit that Nickolas was nothing like Alfred, and her resolve was waning. Kat longed for the feel of his lips on hers and his strong arms around her body.

"Katerina, Mr. Papadopoulos would like to see you." Sophia sang out as she passed Kat at the front desk.

There she was, caught daydreaming about Nickolas again. "Okay, I will head back to his office now. Thank you."

Kat walked through the atrium and down a hallway, her heels clicking on the cobblestone. Finally, she stood in front of his door, smoothed her hands over her dress, took a deep breath, and knocked.

"Come in, Katerina."

"Hello, Mr. Papadopoulos." Nickolas inwardly sighed. He had told her countless times to call him Nickolas, but she wouldn't do it. He thought he saw interest in her eyes, but she built a wall and wouldn't let him in. He tried his hardest to keep it all business, but he knew that was not what it was. He was in love with her. He knew it from the first moment he saw her standing by the check-in desk.

"Katerina, please sit down." He paused while she took her seat, then continued in his forced businesslike manner. "We have an important couple coming from the United States, Mr. and Mrs. Thompson. They own several businesses worldwide and want a place to send their clients and employees for a cultural and fun experience. If they like what we do, they could send a lot of business our way. They will arrive tomorrow morning, and I want the two of us to take them to Santorini and show them the island."

"But Mr. Papadopoulos, I have been leading tours on my own for a month. Is there something wrong?"

"No, not at all. I have gotten glowing reports of your tours. The only reason I would come along is to answer questions regarding the pricing for their clients and make them feel comfortable with our company." He smiled at her, hoping to convey the pride he felt at the job she was doing.

"Okay, thank you. I look forward to meeting them tomorrow."

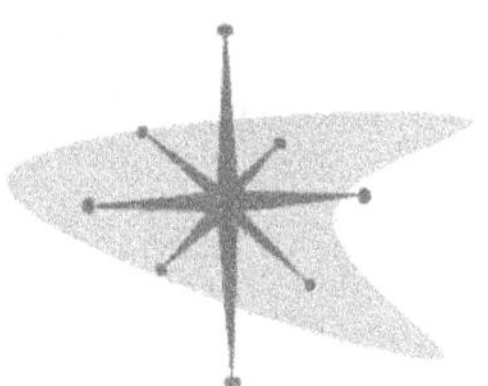

"The iconic island of Santorini, with its unique history, is home to more than two hundred stately churches and monasteries that have stood for centuries. Some enthrall with their traditional architecture, distinguished by whitewashed walls and blue domes, while others have baroque influences. But they all have a distinctive charm that captivates us." Kat was speaking to Mr. and Mrs. Thompson and, of course, Nickolas.

"Well said, my dear," Mrs. Thompson said. Dottie, as she wanted to be called, was a sixty-something fit, blonde woman. She looked to be in her forties but had mentioned how her older grandchildren would love this tour. So far, Kat thought the tour of the churches was going quite well.

"I would love to take my wife for a little walk around the quaint shops if you don't mind. Can we meet you back in front of Saint Spyridon in about an hour?" Mr. Thompson asked.

"That would be fine. We will be right here waiting for you." Nickolas said. The timing couldn't have been more perfect. He wanted some time alone with Kat. He waited until they walked away, then said, "The Thompsons seem to be enjoying themselves."

"Yes, they do. I am glad the tour is going so well."

There was a moment of silence between them that seemed to stretch just a bit too long. Then, finally, Nickolas spoke, "Katerina, you have been with our company for a month. You have to know that I am attracted to you, but more than that, I can see myself building a life with you." He stepped closer to her and leaned in for a kiss, and his world exploded. At last, Nickolas threaded his fingers through her hair and pressed her close against him. For the first time in his life, he was in love.

He dropped to one knee in front of Kat. Her gasp of surprise rang out in front of the church and echoed through the area.

"Katerina Pappas, will you be my wife?"

She smiled and simply said one word: "Yes!"

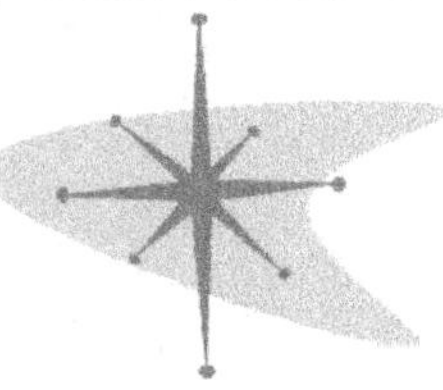

On her wedding day, she looked in the mirror and smiled. She knew she had made the right decision to marry Nickolas, because he proved every day that he loved her.

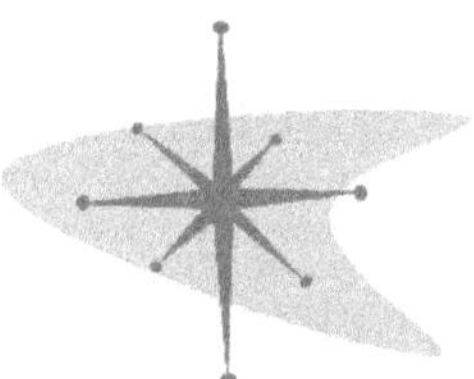

About the Author

Ava Florian Johns writes in the science fiction genre. Her characters are clever and fearless, but in real life, Ava is afraid of her basement, bees, and especially clowns. Truth be told, Ava wouldn't last five minutes in one of her books.

Ava is best known for her Omega Team series.

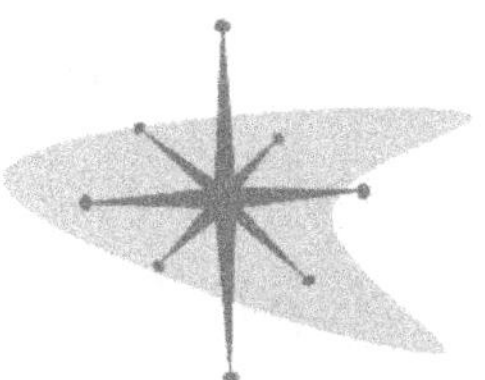

THE HONORABLE COWBOY
by Ann Aubitz

"**A**fter we finish up here, can you please put the lamps in the other cabin, Michael?"

"No problem, I'll run them over, then feed the critters."

Dorothy liked Michaels's soft drawl and how he called the animals critters. Who was she kidding? She just plain liked him. It had been two years since her husband left her a widow at thirty years old. She thought, *Much too young to be alone, but there's no point in getting melancholy now. There's too much work to be done.*

Not only did her husband leave her a widow, but now she was the sole owner of a 2,500-acre ranch in Wyoming. She never wanted to live on a ranch, much less own one. It had been her late husband Jerry's crazy idea. When his grandmother died, he came into some money and decided to invest it in a working ranch. Unfortunately, Jerry didn't know anything about being a cowboy other than what he learned from the movies he watched as a kid. He was obsessed with movies like *Shane* with Alan Ladd and *High Noon,* starring Gary Cooper and Grace Kelly.

So now she was left with this massive piece of land snuggled up against the Big Horn Mountains. The mountains were her favorite part of the whole ranch. She would sit in her Adirondack chair on her porch, look up at the magnificent formations, and know that the mountains would take care of her.

"Dorothy, are you okay?" Michael often worried about her because she would zone out. He didn't know what it was like to lose someone you loved. He had never been in love. A few women said they loved him, but he hadn't been ready to settle down at that point in his life. Now that he was twenty-six, it was time, but the only woman he was interested in was still grieving her late husband. Michael knew he was more than interested in Dorothy. He was in love with her. But he didn't know what to do about it.

"I'm sorry, I'm just gathering wool." She knew that Michael was concerned about her. He couldn't help himself. He was a cowboy through and through—defender of damsels in distress.

"Okay, well, then I'll head out to cabin five and put the lamps away, then go down to the barn to feed the horses. Do you need anything else from me tonight?"

"No, I'll be fine. You can go.

Wow, what a question. Of course, she would love something more from him, but she didn't want to mess with their friendship and working relationship over the last two years. Jerry had hired Michael right before he passed, and Michael had been her rock through it all. It was unusual for a woman in 1968 to own a large ranch, but here she was, and Michael stood by her when she didn't know what to do. He helped her develop a plan for her ranch's future. The idea was to turn this working ranch into a resort, with six cabins for the city slickers to get away and play cowboy for a weekend. After working on the plan for two years, she would open the resort in the spring.

She had enough money left from Jerry's life insurance and the money from the inheritance to live a comfortable life without having to work. But she didn't want to sit on the land and do nothing—it was too beautiful not to share. So, she had Michael teach her every aspect of being a rancher. At first, it was difficult, and every muscle in her body hurt, but how she handled the day-to-day activities like a pro.

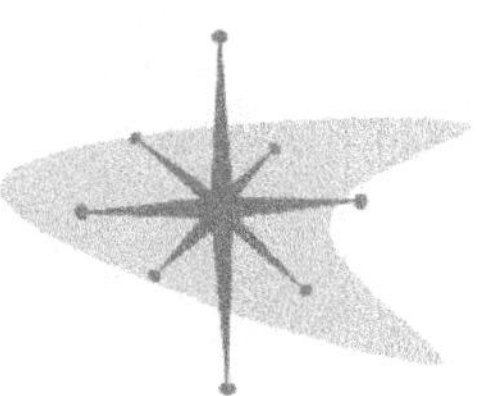

The next day, Dorothy met Michael down at the barn. She was bundled up for a winter's day from head to toe, with only a tuft of blonde hair sticking out from under her hood. She learned quickly that Ohio winters were nothing like the winters in Wyoming. In Wyoming, the landscape was barren, the snow deep, and the winds fierce. So, she learned early on to pile as many clothes on as possible. Luckily, she was never what you would call a fashion plate. She never got into the most updated styles, like shift dresses, miniskirts, and pixie haircuts. She was more into plaid shirts, jeans, and cowboy boots.

She didn't think she looked great in the western wear, but she knew one person that did—Michael. Michael's standard uniform was a western-cut yoked shirt, worn jeans, with cowboy boots and a hat. He filled out the jeans and shirt to perfection. Then, when he would go out on the town, he would wear his fancy black hat and boots. With his dark wavy hair and blue eyes, he looked just like the actors in the cowboy movies her husband used to make her watch.

"Morning, ma'am."

"Good morning, Michael. How are the critters this morning?"

"They're just fine. I was a little worried about Derby's tendon, but he seems okay today."

"That's good news." She took off her gloves and rubbed her hands together to create warmth. "Is there a storm coming today? It feels like it's going to snow."

Michael Smiled. "Spoken like a true Wyoming woman. But, yes, I heard on the radio that the storm would start around three this afternoon. So I'll let the horses out in the pasture, bring them in early, and feed them. Then, if it snows as much as they say it will, I'll string a line to my cabin to get back to the barn."

"What's 'stringing a line'?"

"Oh, sorry, I forgot that we didn't have to do that last winter. It is a rope strung from the barn to one of the houses so we can make it back to take care of the animals. There can be white-out conditions in a blizzard, which can cause us to get disoriented when walking between the buildings. I want to make sure that I can take care of the horses and not get stuck in my cabin or disorientated in the yard."

"Makes sense. Can we string one from the barn to my house? I would feel better if I could help run the ranch instead of staying in my house waiting for the blizzard to end." Dorothy noticed that he smiled again when she said this.

"We can, but we don't have to. I'm sure you have enough to do in the house to keep you busy for a couple of days."

"I do, but I'd like to be able to leave my house if I can. I have never been trapped inside before. The winters in Ohio weren't this severe."

"We also should get you set up in the house if the power goes out."

"Is that a real possibility? I know you told me to buy a generator, but I thought that was for summer storms, not winter storms."

"It's for both. First, we want to make sure you can keep the house heated. My cabin has a fireplace, so I will be okay, but you won't be able to heat your whole house with just the fireplace."

"Okay, well, let's get the horses taken care of and put out to pasture, then we can go in the main house and make sure I am prepared for the storm."

They worked together in a comfortable silence getting the ten horses turned out in record time. Once at the house, Dorothy started to feel nervous about the impending storm. Michael could sense the nervous energy coming off of Dorothy in waves.

"It'll be okay. I promise I won't let anything happen to you."

"I know you'll take care of me, but I keep thinking, what if you weren't here."

"I'm here, and I won't go anywhere."

"That's the same thing that Jerry said to me. And now he is gone, and I am alone."

"You're not alone."

Michael stepped toward her to reassure her that he wasn't going anywhere. She looked so sad. He wished there was something he could do to help her. So he decided to hug her—a hug wouldn't hurt anything.

He reached down and enveloped her in a hug, and she fully accepted it. The heat from their bodies mingled. The hug was friendly and comforting, but then the feeling changed. She looked into his eyes and realized there was more than just friendship. She often wondered what it would be like to be held by him, kissed by him. His muscular arms and strong body. She leaned in, closed her eyes, and waited for him to kiss her. But it never came.

Michael cleared his throat and released her. She instantly felt the loss of the connection.

"I'm going to get the line strung first. Then I will come in and test the generator. If you could, run some water in the tub just in case we need it later."

Dorothy just stared at him. Then, not trusting herself to say anything, she nodded.

He touched two fingers to his hat, turned away from her, and left the house. He wasn't sure what had just happened. The hug that was meant to comfort Dorothy turned into something entirely different.

"Well, that wasn't the smartest thing I've ever done," he said as soon as he walked outside.

Dorothy's face felt hot to the touch. She was in unfamiliar territory. She and Jerry had known each other since they were kids. They grew up in the same neighborhood, attended the same school, and had the same friends. So it was logical to marry him. But her feelings for Michael were anything but logical. Michael started a fire inside her that she had never felt before.

It was said that the 1960s were considered the time of free love, but she just couldn't make herself initiate the first romantic move with Michael. That is just not the way she was. She knew that he liked her, but he was holding back. It may be for the same reason as her. He didn't want to ruin their excellent working relationship.

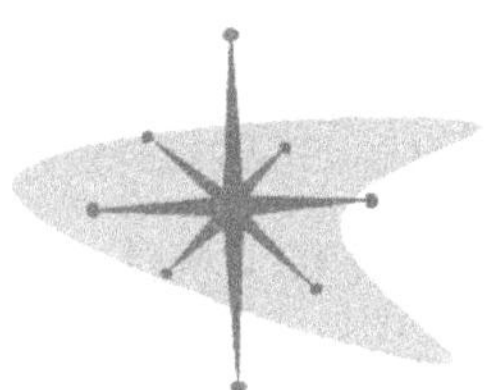

Later that day, as Dorothy was preparing for the storm, Michael came rushing through the door.

"Dorothy, Derby is missing."

"What do you mean missing?"

"He must have gone through the hole in the fence on the north side. The horses never go over there with the snow this deep, so I didn't think I needed to fix it until spring."

"You think he went all the way over to the north fence with his bad leg?"

"That's the only thing I can think of. He may have gotten disoriented in the snow. It is coming down pretty hard."

"Okay, let's go look for him." Dorothy put on her parka, hat, scarf, and mittens.

"I would tell you that you don't have to go out with me, but I don't want to waste time arguing." Michael chuckled.

"Smart man, now let's go get Derby."

Dorothy and Michael had been running the ranch for two years and had never had a horse go outside the fence.

They struggled through the snow toward the north fence. The only thing exposed on either of them was their eyes. Thank goodness they saw Derby standing right outside the fence. He whinnied when they neared him. It was like he was happy to see him.

"Come on, boy, time to get back to the barn." So they turned around and headed toward the barn, fighting every inch of the way through the wind and snow.

They opened the barn door, and the wind took it and slammed it hard against the side of the barn. The hard snow pelted them as they worked together to close the door. They were both breathing hard from the excursion when they closed the door.

"Come on, Derby, let's get you back in your stall, boy." Michael walked with the horse to his stall and grabbed the grooming tote along the way.

"Are you going to groom him now? I thought you would head back to your cabin so you don't get stuck in the barn."

"I wanted the ice and snow out of his coat; then I will get to my cabin. I will be fine, but you should use the line and head to your house."

"Oh, okay." Dorothy was disappointed that Michael wasn't escorting her to her house.

Michael noticed Dorothy's displeasure at his statement. "Or I can walk you back as soon as I am done."

"I would love that." Dorothy smiled. It wasn't as if Dorothy couldn't make it back by herself. She was a very independent woman. She just wanted another opportunity to be alone with Michael.

"Okay, just give me another minute." Just then, all the barn lights flickered twice and went out. "Shoot, we just lost power. I'll wipe down Derby with a towel, then we can head out. The horses will be fine without power, but we need to get your generator running."

They bundled back up in their parkas and headed out into the blizzard. The weather had worsened in the few minutes they were in the barn. Dorothy couldn't even see the outline of the house. She held on to Michael, and he held on to the line that he strung. Thank goodness he got them done before the storm hit.

They burst through the door of her house and tried to keep as much of the snow outside the door as possible. Michael started the generator, but Dorothy thought they should save it when needed. No one knew how long these Wyoming storms would last.

"Let's get into the laundry room and get out of these wet clothes." Dorothy realized how provocative her words sounded, and her face turned bright red. "Sorry, I didn't mean it how it sounded."

Michael cleared his throat. "I knew what you meant."

"Well, I will get us some lunch, and you can start the fire."

"That would be great, thank you."

They had shared lunch many times over the last two years, but it seemed much more intimate today.

"I forgot the power is out on the refrigerator."

"That's okay. Just grab what you need and shut it again." Michael knew that Dorothy typically made sandwiches for lunch.

After a few minutes, Michael had the fire roaring and took the blankets and pillows off the couch so they could sit on the floor. Then, he realized it took Dorothy longer than expected to prepare their lunch, so he got up from his place by the fire and went into the kitchen to find her. He walked into the kitchen, and she was standing by the refrigerator door, holding the cheese and lunchmeat but not moving.

"Dorothy, are you okay?"

"Umm, I'm-I'm okay." She set down the meat and cheese, then wrapped her arms around her body as if trying to stay warm.

"What's wrong? You seem a little bit distracted." Michael's eyes showed concern.

"I am distracted by you." She couldn't believe that she blurted this out to him in the most unromantic way.

"By me? I'm so sorry if I have done something wrong." He was a little confused by her statement but happy as well. She finally seemed like she was ready to be with him.

"You haven't done anything wrong. Michael, it's all me."

Dorothy moved in one fluid step toward Michael and grabbed his face in her hands. She moved toward him and kissed him. Softly at first, then as the surprise faded from Michael, the kiss grew more heated.

"I love you, Dorothy."

"I love you too, my honorable cowboy."

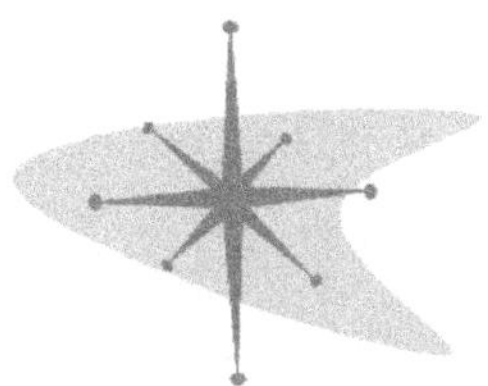

About the Author

Ann Aubitz is the co-owner and publisher of Kirk House Publishers and FuzionPress, located in Burnsville, Minnesota. After years of reading everything she could get her hands on, she decided to help others achieve their dream of becoming an author. Her mission is to help authors reach their goals by seeing their books in print.

Ann is also a proud member of the Independent Book Publishers Association, a board member-at-large for the Midwest Independent Publishers Association, and a group leader for Women of Words (WOW). She also chairs the yearly WOW writing conference.

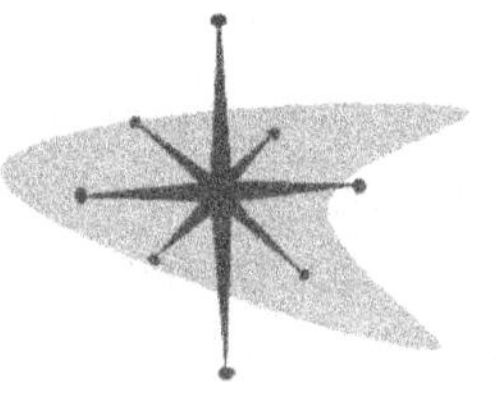

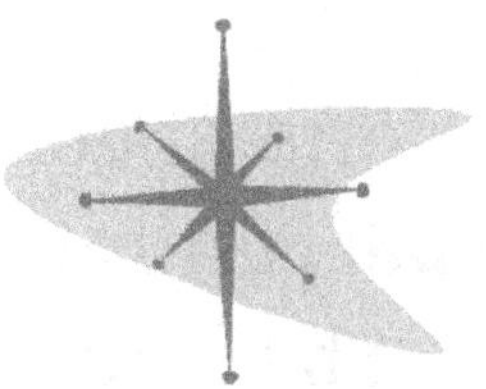

THE CABIN NEXT DOOR

By Susan Schussler

"A car just pulled up at the Larsons' cabin," Mary Louise announced, flipping the old flour-sack dish towel over her shoulder.

"Finally." Valerie dropped the skillet she'd been scrubbing and dried her dishwater-pickled hands on her apron as she rushed to the screen door. She could just make out the silhouettes of four guys and two girls as they climbed out of the green Ford Tudor into the bright midday sun. The land around the lake was mostly farmland, except for the cabin lots, linked by a lonely dirt road. The cabins were close enough to see all ten lots spread along the treeless lakeshore, and the Larsons' place was only a few lots away.

Four years ago, in 1954, Valerie's parents built their three-room cottage, complete with an outside hand pump well and an outhouse. Their summer escape from the city forced Valerie to cultivate a new set of summer friends. Since her dad needed the family car to get to work and only came to the cabin on his days off, Valerie spent her summers with her sister, mother, and the small community around the lake.

Valerie's stomach sank. She couldn't believe her eyes.

"It's Joe and his brothers, but who are the girls?" She hated the jealousy that ratcheted her voice into a squeak. Joe had never brought a girlfriend to the cabin. The lake was special, separate from their identities back in the city. It was her and Joe's place. Valerie knew Joe's parents wouldn't let the boys bring a girl to the cabin unless the relationship was serious—engaged serious—and the thought twisted her insides.

"You don't know that one is with Joe." Mary Louise squeezed between Valerie and the door, blocking her view.

But she did know. Joe was nineteen, and his brothers were too young to get married. Valerie ducked under her sister's arm and balanced on her tiptoes to glimpse the group disappearing behind the tall wood pile near the Larsons' cabin.

"Besides, we need to finish the dishes before Mother and Mrs. Steiner get back from town."

Their mom wouldn't be back for hours, but Valerie finished washing the dishes anyway, happy for the distraction. Still, the women needled her thoughts. She changed into her swimsuit, tying back her dark shoulder-length hair with a red ribbon, then headed for the dock with a towel over her arm. The new red and white Polynesian-inspired two-piece suit from the Montgomery Wards catalog wasn't going to hide in a drawer all summer. She didn't buy it just because Joe Larson's favorite color was red. It was her first two-piece, and it made her feel mature and sexy. If he got engaged over the winter, there was nothing she could do about it but show him what he'd be missing.

Valerie listened to the chatter and laughter as the Larson brothers positioned the family's dock in the lake. The ice had been off the lake for almost two months, but the water was still frigid, so she chuckled under her breath when she heard Joe howl as he waded into the water. It was strange that they were so late installing the dock. Most docks had been in for weeks. The water splashed as they dropped the dock sections into the lake and floated them into place. Next came the pounding. She wasn't going to watch, not if he was engaged. As Valerie closed her eyes, she pictured Joe standing with his shirt off, waist-high in the water, wielding a big hammer to pound the dock poles into the sandy lake bottom, the sinewy muscles of his back flexing with each blow.

She couldn't concentrate on the novel she brought to read with Joe's wet, half-naked body clogging her head, so she closed it. *One Hundred and One Dalmatians*—why couldn't the book be more provocative, like *Breakfast at Tiffany's* or Jack Kerouac's *On the Road*? Valerie stuffed the novel under her towel and flipped onto her back. She couldn't let Joe see her reading a book about puppies.

A loud wolf whistle cut the air, and Valerie glanced toward the Larsons' dock as she sat up, balancing on her elbows. Disappointment filled her as she discovered it wasn't Joe who whistled.

"Looking good, Val." Mike, Joe's younger brother, waved from the water. "We're having a fire tonight. You and Mary Louise should come."

Valerie turned her gaze to Joe, but he fixated on the dock. He wasn't even paying attention to her new suit. She may as well finish her book inside the cabin. She waved to Mike, unsure what to say. She didn't want to go to a bonfire if Joe was going to ignore her.

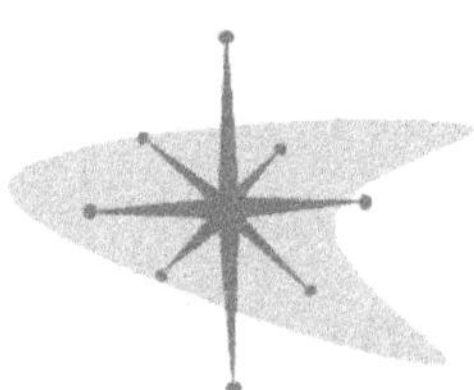

By the time her mother returned, Valerie had finished her book, and dinner needed preparing. Outside at the well, Valerie lifted the red handle of the pump to fill a kettle with water for the potatoes and pushed down, water spurting and splattering her new suit with mud as it hit the ground. *Great.*

Just great. The water flowed better with less air in the pipe on the second pull, so Valerie cupped the chilly water against her suit, trying to remove the mud.

She stopped when she spotted the girls coming out of the Larsons' cabin with Joe and his brothers. The girls were knockouts, a blonde and a brunette. The blonde had short ringlet hair and was stacked like Marilyn Monroe, wearing a low-cut tailored blouse with a short swing skirt. She was next to Joe and probably his girlfriend. The other was skinnier, with long dark hair, wearing pedal pushers and a blouse tied at her midriff. How was she supposed to compete with Marilyn Monroe and Audrey Hepburn? Valerie filled the pot with water and headed back into the cabin, more determined than ever to skip the bonfire.

During dinner, Valerie couldn't focus. Her thoughts kept drifting back to last year's end of season bonfire, the night Joe kissed her. When Joe Larson slipped his hand around hers and pulled her onto his lap, she thought he'd belong to her forever. His fingers combed through her hair as his eyes met hers, and then his lips pressed against her, taking and giving all at the same time. It was the best kiss she'd ever had.

He'd always been the quiet brother, the intellectual one, and it took her an entire summer to get him to talk to her. But once she did, they talked about everything from their childhoods to their futures. Joe had gotten accepted into the university and planned to study mechanical engineering. The inner workings of industrial machines had captivated him since he was a child, and he didn't want to be stuck on an assembly line like his dad. Valerie planned to finish school and get a job at the local bank her uncle managed. They'd have the summer together before she started at the bank and he returned to school. She always thought Joe would wait for her to finish high school. But he must have met the girl at college, and now, he was engaged.

"Mrs. Steiner said Elmer Larson had a heart attack last fall at work. That must be why the boys are so late getting the dock into the water." Valerie's mother interrupted her thoughts.

"A heart attack? Is he all right?" Joe's dad was one of the strongest men she knew. *Why didn't Joe tell me?* Oh, that's right, he was ignoring her because he was engaged to another woman.

"He won't be able to return to his old job, but the union is helping him find work at the plant. Mrs. Steiner said they almost had to sell their cabin to make ends meet, but Joe wouldn't hear of it. The union got Joe a job on the line. He's supporting the whole family by the sounds of it."

Poor Joe. His dad's heart attack decimated his plans to be an engineer, and now, he was stuck on the assembly line just like his dad. No wonder Joe hadn't called on her all winter. He was too busy working to support his family.

"The Larsons are having a bonfire tonight, Mother. I think Mary Louise and I should go?" Valerie needed to talk to Joe, and the bonfire could be her last chance. "Just to make sure Mr. Larson is better."

Her mom's lips pursed as if debating the request, but a smile lurked underneath. "Have fun, but stay out of trouble."

The fading sun streaked orange across the dark blue water when Valerie and Mary Louise stepped out into the mosquito-infested air and headed for the Larsons' lakeshore. Four roughly made log benches surrounded a ring of large stones with logs stacked inside. Valerie sat on the bench next to the blonde. She figured she might as well introduce herself. Joe stood in front of them, blowing on the kindling, trying to get the fire to catch on the wood, his back to them.

"Hi, I'm Valerie." She held her hand out to the blonde.

The blonde smiled, her white teeth and perfect cherub red lips mocking Valerie. "Oh, I know who you are. Joe's told me all about you. I'm Paula."

The blonde's words unsettled Valerie, and she didn't know what to say. What had Joe told her? Just then, Joe's head slowly turned, noticing Valerie for the first time, his eyes wide with uneasiness.

Joe looked to his brother Mike and back at the two women. Mike lifted his chin encouragingly and then got up to help light the fire. When the fire caught, and flames lapped the edges of the logs, Joe squeezed between the women on the bench. Valerie's heart broke as she felt his heat against her skin. He smelled of all the good cabin smells—fresh air, burning wood, and, best of all, the wholesome clean scent of Joe Larson. Coming here was a mistake. Valerie needed to say her condolences and go home.

"I'm sorry about what happened to your dad. It must have been hard on your family. Is he feeling any better?" She wanted to ask whether he would be able to go to college in the fall or if he planned to keep working on the line, but what was the use? His plans no longer involved her. She had no right to pry.

"Yeah. Thanks," Joe said in his soft baritone.

The blonde touched Joe's knee. "You should take Val for a walk so you can talk."

Joe nodded. "Yeah. I should." He turned to Valerie. "Will you walk with me?"

Valerie stood, knowing what was coming. He'd tell her how sorry he was, but he was in love with Paula, and they were getting married. Valerie ambled toward the road. The sun was setting, and they only had about twenty minutes before it got dark. It wouldn't be a long conversation. Really, it was commendable of the blonde to let him give her closure, to let her down easy.

Joe walked alongside her with his hands in his pockets, not talking. She'd never seen him so nervous. Joe Larson was a nice guy, quiet and kind. She felt guilty making him suffer now.

"I know what you're going to say."

"You do?" He stopped and turned to her. "I…it's just that with what happened to my dad, I realized how short life is, and I—"

"You don't have to explain." She started walking again. "I understand. She's a great girl. I mean, she has to be if you fell in love with her."

"Fell in love with her?"

"Yeah, how could you not? She's gorgeous."

"Who?" Joe's brows furrowed.

"Paula, the Marilyn Monroe look-a-like. I'm not stupid, Joe." Her pace picked up as she struggled not to cry. "I figure you must be engaged to bring her to the cabin, and you have my blessing. Really, you do. With your dad sick and all, I understand. You couldn't wait for me to finish high school. You needed to start your life. I just want you to be happy, Joe. You deserve to be happy." Valerie couldn't stop the tears from pooling in her eyes.

Joe stopped in the middle of the road and reached for her hand, but she couldn't let him see her cry and kept walking. She was ten feet ahead of him by the time he yelled.

"Val. Val, would you stop?"

She stopped but couldn't turn to face him.

"I'm not marrying Paula."

"Well then, Audrey Hepburn. I'm sure she's equally as great."

"I'm not marrying her either."

Valerie's breath hitched, and she wiped her eyes before turning around. Joe strode toward her. His serious blue eyes fixed on her brown ones.

"But, Paula knows all about us."

When he reached her, he crouched to get eye level. "She does." His thumb gently swept beneath her eyes before he pulled her into a hug. "But not for the reason you think. Paula's my cousin. I told her about you."

A sob caught in her throat.

"But you've been avoiding me. Why have you been avoiding me?"

"I'm nervous." He pulled back and looked her straight in the eyes. "With all that's happened with my dad, I'm nervous, okay? My whole life's been derailed, and I've got to help my family. It won't be forever because my dad's starting a new job soon. But I'm nervous because I heard you had a boyfriend and went to spring formal with him, and I never told you how I felt. I'm in love with you, Valerie Marie Penske, and the thought of us together is the only thing that's gotten me through the winter. I need to know you love me too and that I haven't screwed up by waiting so long to tell you."

She had gone to spring formal, but it wasn't with anyone special, no one like Joe. It was her senior year. Was she not supposed to go? She and Joe hadn't talked about going steady. She wasn't sure where she stood with him.

"Wait a minute. You were worried that I had found someone else?"

He nodded.

"Say that part about loving me again."

"I love you, Valerie."

He loved her. How had she gotten it all wrong?

"Oh, Joe, I love you too. It's always been you."

Joe pushed a lock of her hair back, tucking it behind her ear as his gaze penetrated her. Then his lips were on hers, and Valerie's entire body lit with tingling butterflies. *He loved her.* He pulled her closer, and as her arms draped around his neck, he lifted her. Her legs wrapped around his waist as he trailed kisses down her neck.

A whoop called from somewhere in the dark, and they glanced up to see a straight line of sight between where they stood, kissing, and the fire pit.

"Guess the answer's yes," Mike yelled across the span.

Joe lowered Valerie to the ground and kissed her once more before answering his brother. "I haven't asked her yet, stupid."

"Will you marry me?" He dropped to one knee and pulled a gold ring with five small stones from his pocket, holding it up for her inspection. "It was my grandmother's, and we can't get married right away, not until my dad's working full-time, but..."

It was the prettiest ring she'd ever seen. "Yes," Valerie said as she plucked it from his fingers and slid it onto her left hand.

Joe yelled to the group at the fire, "She said yes," and everyone hollered with excitement.

They walked to the end of the road, talking, and when Joe slipped his hand around hers, Valerie knew no matter what life threw at them, she and Joe would always have each other.

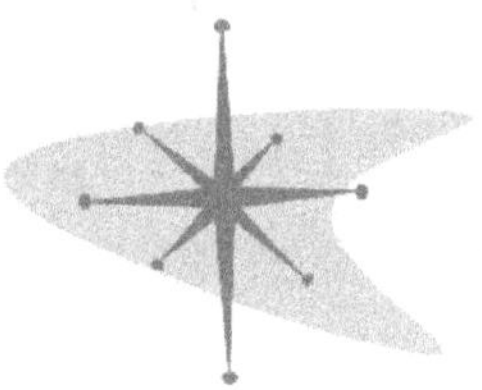

About the Author

Susan Schussler writes realistic love stories full of twists and turns. Inspired by years of working directly with others in nutrition and nursing, her characters often resemble the girl next door or someone you'd swear you know from school. Her first book, *Between the Raindrops*, debuted in 2013, and she's been writing novels ever since.

Schussler lives in Minnesota with her husband and children. And though she hates to admit it, when she's not writing or on one of Minnesota's gorgeous lakes, you may find her catching up on celebrity news.

Find her online at https://susanschussler.com

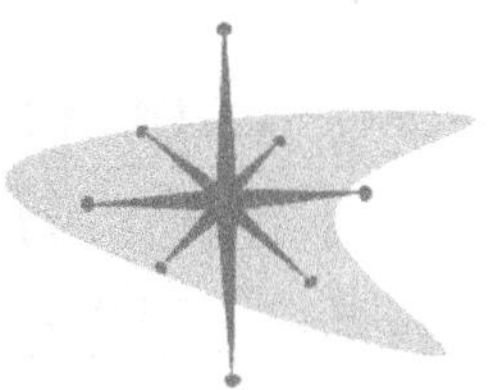

A Second Prom for Maureen

By Leandra Logan

The lunch hour at Monroe High School was in full swing. Stationed at the food service counter, scooping cheesy casserole onto student plates, Maureen Conway Bennett had a front-row ticket to the friendly chaos.

"It's her!'

"No."

"Maybe…"

The snippet of conversation that caught Maureen's attention today was coming from a table of popular girls, cheerleaders, to be precise. And to her surprise, the cheerleaders seemed to be staring in her direction!

So many things had changed at Monroe High since her four-year tenure here a dozen years ago. Since the days of poodle skirts, tightly curled hair, bobby socks in saddle shoes, and button-down sweaters.

Today, in the accelerated whirlwind of 1966, the girls wore short floral shifts that barely cleared their tushes, maintained long sheets of hair, and preferred bare feet in comfy sandals.

This freestyle behavior greatly appealed to Maureen, who, at age thirty, retained the heart of a teenager. She was certainly older and infinitely wiser now, but deep inside, she was still a girl full of dreams and schemes.

As the cheerleaders continued to stare, she wondered: Had they discovered who she was?

The very idea of discovery triggered her defenses. She currently portrayed a rather unflattering picture in her white nylon service uniform, with her blond tresses balled up under a hairnet.

Her anonymity hadn't bothered her in her two months of employment in the school kitchen. She was, after all, on a journey of self-discovery and enjoyed being little more than a Jetson's robot in students' eyes for the time being.

Maureen needed time to grow and heal, and the best place for it seemed to be her hometown of Willow Springs, California, especially as she was flat broke and again living with her parents.

Maureen was only mildly surprised when the four cheerleaders returned to the cafeteria after school. She was working alone back in the kitchen, slicing long pans of cherry

Jell-O into cubes for tomorrow's dessert, when she heard their stage whispers in the dining area. In a burst of excitement, they pushed through the swinging door, dressed in blue-and-gold cheerleader uniforms. Their hemlines were shorter, but the overall look hadn't changed much since she'd headed the Monroe Bulldog squad.

"Mrs. Bennett?"

Maureen stilled her plastic knife and flashed them a bright smile. "How can I help?"

"Are you her? I mean…"

"Are you *that* Maureen?"

"The legend…"

Maureen chuckled. "Well, I am Maureen Conway. And I did lead your squad back in fifty-four."

"And you were prom queen, right? We spotted your photographs in the hallway and noted the resemblance."

Maureen's confidence faded as they assessed her, taking in the red and orange smears on her top. She felt her reputation as Maureen 'Cool Cat' Conway was unexpectedly being washed down the drain!

No way could she be meeting their lofty expectations in her current condition.

She knew this because she had once been one of them, a privileged girl who was, at times, impatient, quick to judge, slow to forgive.

To Maureen's surprise, the foursome continued to smile at her, if not with reverence, at least with a measure of expectation.

Jeanie, the squad captain, spoke up. "We're thinking of forming a prom committee."

A prom committee in March? That seemed to be cutting it fine. Most committees typically started working on events in autumn, especially the formal dances.

"It's hard to know," Jeanie said, "exactly how to begin. But surely, as a former queen, you have ideas."

"It was so long ago. So much has changed, from clothing to music to decoration." Maureen sat at the table. "Wouldn't it be better to speak to last year's seniors? They must have the scoop on how to host the event."

"You don't understand," Jeanie bemoaned. "This school no longer does prom!"

"We're trying to bring it back," a redheaded cheerleader added.

The girls paced the kitchen, fuming over its unfairness.

"It's all Old Man Hen—Mr. Henshaw's fault. He is such a square."

Maureen agreed but was determined to stay neutral about her employer.

The shortest cheerleader piped up. "My mom says fun things vanish when school funding dries up."

Maureen nodded. "Makes sense."

The girls settled against the counters, focusing on Maureen. "Do you have any ideas, Mrs. Bennett?"

Maureen paused. "Well, you could poll the students and teachers to determine interest, then circulate Rescue Prom petitions. Lots of signatures might help sway Mr. Henshaw."

Jeanie snapped her fingers. "Yes! We could also make some posters to spread the word."

Maureen beamed. It felt surprisingly good to be consulted.

"With Mr. Henshaw's approval, you could offer to do fundraisers to pay expenses. Plus, couples pay for tickets; there's another source of income."

The girls gasped when Cello Dave, the school's band teacher, breezed into the kitchen in a trendy suit, his hair flopping slightly on his forehead. "Cello Dave!" they chorused.

"Hello, ladies!" He dove into the large refrigerator to pluck out a sandwich wrapped in wax paper and two small milk cartons. "Thanks for saving my lunch, Maur—Mrs. Bennett," he swiftly corrected.

The girls grinned. He'd nearly called the lunch lady by her first name! How lucky was she!

Maureen beckoned him over to her table. "Cello Dave sometimes skips lunch to tutor band students."

Maureen's heart did a flip-flop. Dave was approximately her age of thirty and sinfully handsome. A man to be truly admired, powerful in principle. Somehow, he'd successfully breached Mr. Henshaw's rules for formality in class, encouraging the kids to call him by a too-cool-for-school nickname! Dave insisted it garnered him respect and made him far more approachable to the shy kids often drawn to band. Furthermore, behind his trendy style, he was a serious musician who could play several instruments. A fully qualified mentor.

The school grapevine crackled with tidbits about the bachelor, his '64 Mustang, and his bungalow near the school, where he often gave one-man cello concerts from his front porch.

Why hadn't he been around in 1954 when Maureen had the senior class by the string, was herself playing cello in the band, and falling for loser Wade Bennett?

Meanwhile, Dave had joined Maureen and was digging into his sandwich and milk.

"Did I interrupt something?" he asked.

The girls openly swooned at his interest. Maureen tried to play it cool. "The girls are anxious to bring back prom."

"From positive extinction!" Jeanie exclaimed.

Cello Dave choked a little on his sandwich. Maureen patted him on the back, and he gulped some milk.

Jeanie continued. "It occurred to us that Mrs. Bennett, being an alum, might have some suggestions on how to approach Old Man—"

"Careful," Dave interrupted.

"Whatever Mr. Henshaw's reasons were for canceling the event in the first place, I imagine he'll be most receptive if you approach him with courtesy and initiative." Maureen measured Cello Dave's frown. "Are you okay?"

Dave addressed the girls. "Mrs. Bennett has only worked here a couple of months. You shouldn't put her on the spot."

Jeanie drew close to Cello Dave. "You know, with your popularity around this outdated museum, maybe *you* could lead our Rescue Prom committee."

"Whoa!" Cello Dave raised his palms in the air.

Maureen intervened with a laugh. "Cello Dave is already a busy man. No, the best place to start is probably with your mothers. Speak to them this weekend."

With a tug of blue-and-gold sweater and a bounce of the pleated skirt, the cheerleaders cheerily exited. "Rally your mothers!" Maureen good-naturedly repeated.

Dave stood and tossed his trash.

"Seems pretty crazy, canceling a big event like prom," Maureen pondered.

"A real shame," Cello Dave agreed.

"Were you teaching here when it happened?"

He appeared startled by the question. "No. I wasn't teaching here." He quickly moved for the swinging door. "Thanks for the afterschool snack."

"Anytime, Dave. Anytime."

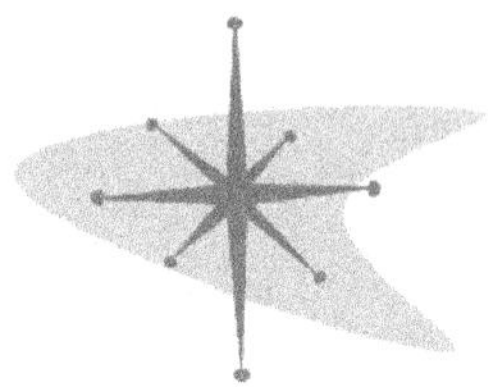

Weekends were particularly awkward for Maureen, again living out of her childhood bedroom, contending with her parents' routine and expectations. They still cared but had never forgiven her for eloping with the class jerk-jock and abandoning her comfortable life in California to live hand-to-mouth with Wade in Arizona. Her big brother was the family's star, a married pediatrician.

It would take time, but Maureen was determined to win back her parents' trust and admiration.

As usual, Monday couldn't come too soon.

As was her custom, Maureen got to school early and slipped into Cello Dave's classroom to monitor early morning band practice. Dave was working on a delightful arrangement of *Back to School* by Bo Diddley. She was flooded with memories of her time here as a cellist. A gangly boy who could barely balance the cello between his legs now occupied her seat. But he was just as committed as she had been, his head tilted as he drew the bow over the strings. When the song ended, he leaned over to converse with the pretty girl seated next to him, making her laugh.

More déjà vu. Maureen also had a cello buddy, Billy. He had been small like this boy, quiet and shy. But, somehow, Billy had mustered the nerve to befriend her, a popular cheerleader. Maureen realized it was one of the most genuine relationships of her life. She often thought of Billy, how he must hate her even after all these years.

The musical hour passed quickly. Maureen was due in the cafeteria to begin the luncheon setup. As she retraced her steps to the front of the school, Maureen noticed a flurry of activity in the halls. Gaily-colored posters endorsing prom were tacked-up everywhere, and the cheerleaders circulated with clipboards, encouraging students to sign their petitions to resurrect the formal dance.

When the cheerleaders noticed Maureen, they joyously surrounded her as if she'd arrived not in her white uniform but in a Cinderella ballgown.

Maureen anxiously pressed a hand to her heart. "But I didn't do anything!"

"Didn't you?"

Maureen whirled to discover Mr. Henshaw standing in the doorway of the school offices. The principal was furious.

More déjà vu. Maureen hadn't seen him this angry since the day he'd expelled her back in 1954, two weeks before graduation.

"My office, Maureen. Now."

Preparing to take the walk of shame of yesteryear, Maureen instinctively folded into a teenage slouch as she moved through the reception area and into Mr. Henshaw's inner sanctum.

The principal didn't invite Maureen to sit as he rounded his desk to take his chair. But Maureen suddenly felt defiant, a thirty-year-old adult with no current scandals to defend. She took a chair opposite him with her chin held high.

Mr. Henshaw pounded his desk. "*Now,* what are you trying to pull, Maureen?"

"Nothing—"

"I gave you this job out of the goodness of my heart because I believe in second chances. And what do you do? Incite a rebellion over a silly dance!"

"Prom is not silly. But I am not to blame—" Maureen cut herself short when she heard the door click. Cello Dave had entered! How she hated for Dave to see her in this humiliating battle.

Mr. Henshaw scowled. "I didn't send for you."

"No, sir, you didn't. But Maury is telling it straight."

Maury. Nobody had called Maureen Maury since she'd been a student here. She rather liked it coming from Dave.

Cello Dave cleared his throat and loosened his tie. "Mrs. Bennett was working in the kitchen, minding her own business when the girls came to consult her about resurrecting prom. They recognized her as a former prom queen and believed she might help."

"Precisely! I merely suggested they revive interest by circulating petitions. But I also suggested they consult their mothers first."

Mr. Henshaw's glare deepened as if she hadn't spoken. "You've got a nerve, Maureen. After all the trouble you caused at *your* prom—"

"I am so sorry for what happened back then." Maureen could feel tears sting her eyes as a wave of humiliation surged through her. There'd been a skirmish at the 1954 dance near the hotel's fountain. Her boyfriend Wade Bennett had been roaring drunk and wrenched her by the arm when she'd danced with her cello partner, Billy Davidson. The tough football player had then effortlessly tossed spindly Billy into the fountain, which ignited a free-for-all that landed several students in the gushing waters.

Right here in this office the following Monday morning, Maureen and Wade had been expelled.

"Sure, we were dumb kids. But you, sir, were in charge. Despite his value as the school's star quarterback, the faculty must've long realized what a troublemaker Wade was. The chaperones should've tossed him out hours earlier." Maureen halted on a tearful sniff, then flashed Cello Dave a smile as he handed her a tissue.

"Wade alone was responsible for what happened," Cello Dave asserted. "Losing the prom king vote was enough to set him off. He was like a raging bull."

Maureen noted that Dave was suddenly quite flushed. She dazedly wondered how he knew so much about Wade's antics.

"As for the current bid for prom," Maureen continued, "would it be so bad to reinstate the event? Now the girls believe it has to do with lack of funding—" She hesitated in bewilderment as Cello Dave cleared his throat. "Surely, some hasty fundraisers could quickly build up the kitty."

Mr. Henshaw's nostrils flared, and his eyes grew wide. "You still don't get it, do you?"

"Mr. Henshaw," Cello Dave began.

The principal waved him off. "Maureen, you and Wade are the sole reason there is no prom to this day."

"What!"

"That's right, young lady. I outlawed prom the minute you and your loser boyfriend left the building."

"You can't mean it!"

"So perhaps, finally, you can see why I find your meddling most distasteful and presumptuous. The girls will soon find out exactly what you did and why there is no prom, on that I can guarantee."

"That's pretty spiteful," Dave admonished.

"Watch your step, Mr. Davidson," Mr. Henshaw cautioned. "I acknowledge the power of your teaching skills and popularity, but I have my limits."

"Mr. Davidson?" Maureen's jaw dropped. Monroe High's current dreamboat was *her* Billy Davidson? The scrawny musician who'd stood up to Wade? "I simply can't believe it! I feel so foolish!"

"Maury, please—"

With a helpless flutter of hands, Maureen dashed out of the office and out of the school.

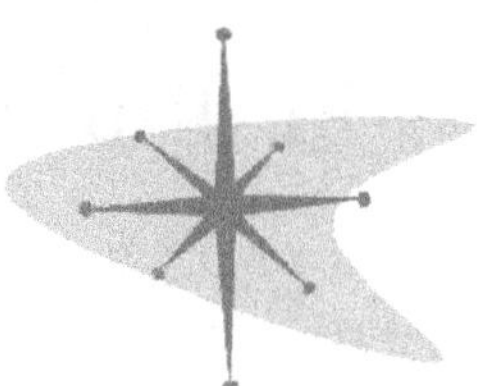

Maureen could hear Billy Davidson's cello music drifting through the air that evening as she traipsed down the sidewalk to his house. It had been a while since she'd toted around her cello, but soon it felt right at home strapped to her back.

She tentatively mounted the steps of his front porch, sat beside him on a wooden chair, and removed her cello from its case. As in the past, he silently waited as she got the instrument into position. Then together, they began to play their favorite duet of yesteryear: *Misty*. Several more duets followed. Neighbors lingered outside, applauding in gratitude.

Later, over a bottle of their favorite, Hires Root Beer, Maureen was ready to talk.

"I've thought of you so often, Billy, all the fun we shared playing beautiful music, our thrilling concerts. And our dreamy dance at the prom, to Misty... I briefly fancied us together before Wade tore you away."

"You should've said, Maury. You should've chosen me!"

"I wasn't mature enough. I was a silly girl who loved being popular. But I grew up fast in Arizona, married to an angry drunk with no ambition. We divorced within four months." Maureen shook her head in disbelief. "You know, I didn't recognize you at all!"

"I was determined to reinvent myself," Cello Dave confided proudly. "I studied music and teaching in college, worked out in the gym. Then I came home to do what I love most, make music."

"I guess when people follow their dreams, they do become their best self. So, you prefer Dave to Billy now?"

"Very much. Cello Dave is a nickname I picked up during my first year of teaching, and I feel it fits my fresh start perfectly. As for fresh starts, it's not too late to chase your old dream, Maury, go to college."

"Oh, but I did go. Worked my way through university after the divorce. I also have a degree in teaching."

"Then why take the cafeteria job?"

"Because I wanted to return to our school for a little while, feel a part of it again. I was forced out so abruptly. I longed for some closure. Besides, you can't seriously imagine Mr. Henshaw offering me a teaching position, especially in the spring."

"You should have come home straight after the divorce, Maury."

"I didn't think I'd be welcomed home, especially by you. Oh, why didn't you just tell me you were Billy? Finding out from Henshaw was so humiliating."

"I planned to tell you. I just hoped you might fall in love with me first, fall in love with popular Cello Dave."

Stunned, Maureen's heart swelled with pleasure. "You needn't have bothered to make yourself over for me. I've known for quite some time you were the true love that got away."

"I never stopped loving you either, Maury."

"A second chance with you is a dream come true," she whispered shyly.

"Seems we're meant to be." Dave leaned over and kissed her. "Now, how would you feel about a new nickname of your own?"

"Like what?"

"Mrs. Cello Dave Davidson. We've lost enough time as it is."

"I say, let's play to that!"

They contentedly shifted their cellos back into position. "Can we possibly rescue prom for those kids, Dave?"

"Consider it done. I spoke to Henshaw after school, after he'd cooled down, and made a case for it."

Maureen knowingly sized him up. "Did you threaten to quit?"

"Of course. And it worked. There will be a prom, and we are heading the planning committee."

"Happy days are here again, Cello Dave."

"Yes, Maury, the happiest of days."

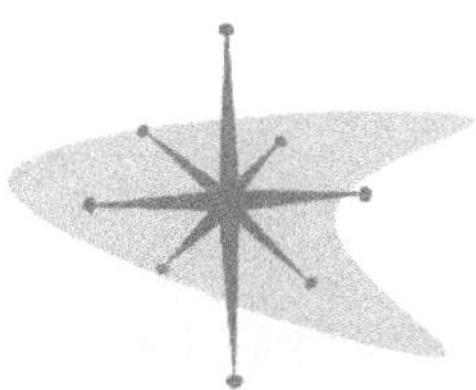

About the Author

Mary Jane Schultz often writes under the penname Leandra Logan. She is a multi-published, bestselling author in various genres, including romance, mystery, young adult, and illustrated books for children. Mary Jane is a Romantic Times Awards winner and has received numerous nominations within the industry. Her critics praise her for her deeply emotional stories, often lightened with humor, and the red herrings she thoroughly enjoys planting to keep her readers guessing.

Mary Jane resides in the historic town of Stillwater, Minnesota.

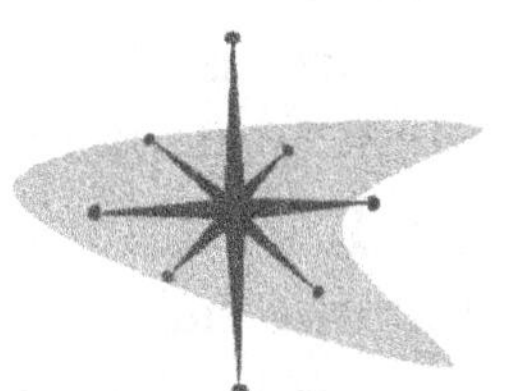

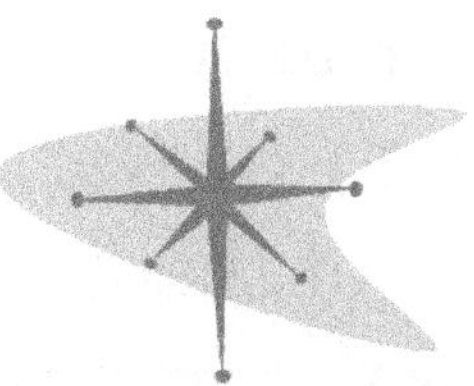

DRAFTED FOR LOVE

Love Promises Collection
By C. Kelly

"Gigi, what's in this box?" Izzy asked as she stepped out of the basement stairwell.

"Oh my goodness, I haven't seen that box in years," Great Grandma Irene, or Gigi as Izzy liked to call her, answered. "It's full of love promises."

"Love promises?"

"Did I tell you the story of when your great-grandfather Ethan was sent off to war?"

Izzy shook her head. "Please tell me."

Izzy watched as her great-grandmother got a far-off look on her face and started to reminisce about her husband, Ethan. Gigi always got that look on her face when she thought about her husband of sixty-two years.

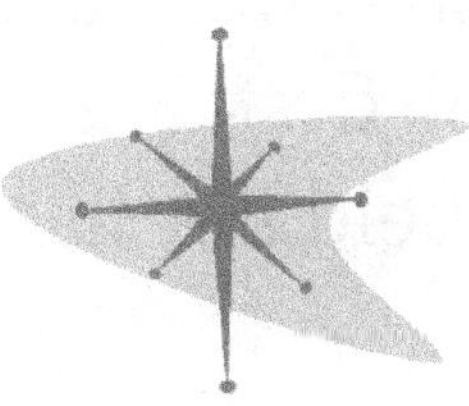

It was early 1942, Pearl Harbor had just been bombed, and the US was preparing to go to war. The draft notices were issued, and Ethan was one of the first to receive one. He had recently moved to town to start his job as a mechanic for Hudson's Garage. They had only been dating for three months. She couldn't believe he was going off to war. She was so afraid something would happen to him, and he would never come home.

The night before he was to board a bus, they went out to eat at Clark's diner.

"I'm gonna miss you, Irene. I can't believe I leave tomorrow already."

"I can't believe you leave tomorrow, either. It sure is going to be lonely around here without you, Duckie."

"Now, I want you to promise me something, Dove."

"What's that?"

"I don't want you to forget about me while I'm gone."

"Oh, Ethan, how could I ever forget about you?"

They finished their dinner, and as Ethan paid for their meal, he asked, "Will you go for a walk with me?"

"Sure."

He reached down and clasped her hand in his. She felt her heart start to flutter. He had held her hand before, but every single time was just like the first. Her heart never failed to beat harder in her chest as he held her hand.

They strolled down Main Street. It was late April. The spring air was warm, but the breeze still had a bite to it. Irene shivered. Ethan stopped, slid his jacket off, and draped it over her shoulders. She smiled at him. At that moment, she felt so cherished. They continued to slowly stroll down the sidewalk hand in hand. Neither one wanted the night to end.

"Let's go sit at the park." Irene nodded her head in agreement.

Once they sat, Ethan turned to her and gently cupped her cheek.

"Irene, I was serious about you not forgetting about me while I'm gone."

"Ethan Denton. How can you possibly think I could ever forget about you? We spend every minute we can together. When you leave, I'm going to be just lost without you. Who will I talk to? Who will walk with me? Who can I share a root beer float with?"

"No one," he quickly interjected. "Absolutely no one, besides me, of course."

She smiled. "Of course."

He leaned into her and pressed his lips to hers.

"I love you, Irene," he stated firmly but softly.

"Oh, Ethan, I love you, too," she quickly replied.

"I know it's too soon for me to tell you that I love you, but I didn't want to leave without you knowing how I truly felt. You are it for me, Dove."

"You're it for me, too, Duckie."

"Come on, as much as I don't want this night to end, I need to get you back home before your folks start to worry."

They both stood. Gigi took a step and looked down at her feet. Her shoelaces had come untied. Ethan looked down at her feet and smiled.

"Dove, your shoes are untied again."

"Yes, I realize that."

"I think your shoes have come untied on every date we've ever had. If I didn't know better, I'd think you were untying them on purpose."

She giggled. "I'm not untying them, I promise!"

He laughed with her.

"Let me tie your shoe." Just as he had on every date previously, he knelt down and tugged on the laces to tighten them up before he tied them. Just as he pulled, the lace in his right hand broke. He looked down at the broken cord he held in his hand.

"Well, this will make tying your shoes a bit of a challenge."

"Oh, no, what happened?"

"I guess I've tied your shoes with these laces one too many times. Let me unlace the string a couple of holes."

He proceeded to work the remaining shoelace through the holes until it was even on both sides. Then, finally, he tied her shoe, albeit higher up on her foot.

"There. That should at least get us to your house."

He stood up with the broken piece in his hand. He looked down at his hand, then up at her face. He cautiously reached out his hand and caught her left hand in his own. He intently looked into her eyes once again.

She swallowed. "Ethan?"

"I love you, Irene. More than I ever believed was possible. I know you are the woman for me. I have known it from almost the day we met." He took the broken piece of shoelace and carefully tied it around her ring finger on her left hand.

"Mind you, I'm not proposing. Not yet. I can't do that until I ask for your father's permission, but I'm making a promise to you that when I return from the war, I will ask for your hand, and we will be married. If that's what you want."

"Yes, oh Ethan, yes. That's what I want."

"When you look at this broken piece of string, know that is how I'm feeling. I'll be broken until we're reunited."

He leaned forward and gently placed a kiss on her lips.

"Come on, let me get you home."

They quietly walked hand in hand back to her house. Both lost in their thoughts. They walked up her front steps. He once again gently held her cheek and leaned in for one final kiss.

"I love you, Irene."

"I love you, too, Ethan. I will pray for your safe return. Please come home to me."

"I promise to do everything in my power to come home to you so we can start our life together."

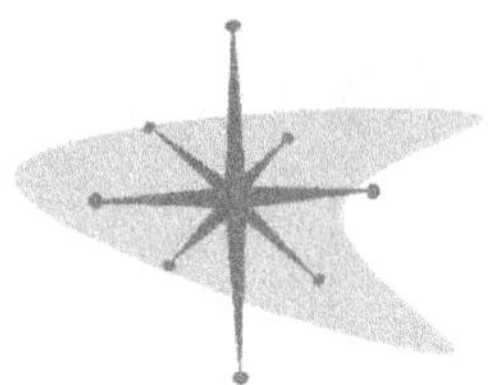

"Gigi, that is the most romantic story I have ever heard!"

"I still have the tied piece of string in my jewelry box."

"Of course you do. It was the promise ring Great-Grandpa Ethan gave to you."

"Yes, it was." Gigi smiled a sweet smile. In her smile, Izzy could see all of the years of love and laughter that her great-grandparents had shared up until Great-Grandpa Ethan had passed away some ten years ago.

"While I loved hearing your story, I don't understand what it has to do with this box?"

"After your great-grandfather left, I looked at that piece of shoelace wrapped around my finger and thought about him every day. Of course, I prayed God would keep him safe. But, I also prayed he wouldn't forget me."

"How could he forget you?"

"He was off doing who knows what. There was nothing there to remind him of me. While I was here every day with constant reminders of him, I knew it wasn't the same for him. Walking down the street where we had walked reminded me of him. Sitting in the drug store drinking a root beer float brought him to mind. He didn't have any of those things.

"So about a week after he left, I was relacing my shoe when I decided I should send him a keepsake, something to remind him of me. Nothing valuable. Not that I had anything valuable to send him anyway. I just wanted to send him—"

"You sent him the other half of the broken shoelace," Izzy guessed.

Gigi smiled and nodded. "I sent him the other half of my broken shoelace."

"It was no small feat. I'll tell you. I went to the recruiting office to ask how I could send a letter to him. The man working the office told me the draftees were being sent to different bases all over the country for basic training. He then asked if I knew where Ethan had been sent. I told him he was sent to Fort Benning. He said that probably meant that Ethan was drafted into the army and may likely end up in Europe, but he couldn't be sure. He then handed me two preprinted sheets of stationary and told me once I knew where he was stationed, I could write him a letter on the special paper. The US military had started a new mail system. It was called V-mail, for Victory mail. The army postal office handled over twenty million pieces of mail each week. The military had created a system where you wrote a letter on their special stationery. The letters would be copied onto reels of microfilm. The reels, which were like the old movie pictures, would be shipped to the postal station wherever the men were stationed. Each letter was reprinted and given to the individual serviceman."

"Oh my gosh, Gigi. That sounds incredible! I've never heard of that."

"It was quite genius. It allowed the US to send thousands of letters over on a single reel of film, saving both space on the plane and, more importantly, weight."

"But, Gigi, if they filmed the letter, how could you send the shoelace?"

"That was the problem I had. I knew I couldn't use the V-mail system to send my keepsake to Ethan. I had to find a different way. I could have sent it through the regular mail system once Ethan gave me his address, but I heard the news reports about the importance of using V-mail over regular mail to aid in the war effort. I felt guilty sending my letter with the shoelace using the regular mail system, knowing it would take up valuable space on a supply plane. There were also care packages you could buy to send to your serviceman. However, many of these were pre-packaged, and you couldn't add something to them."

"What did you do?"

"I prayed God would help me find a way to get my love promise to Ethan, which He did." She smiled her sweet smile once again.

"How did you get it to Great-Grandpa?"

"I was at the drugstore having a root beer float, thinking of Ethan, when Alice Corner walked in. She sat down next to me and started to cry. I asked her what was wrong. She told me her brother Stuart had just received a draft notice. I told her I knew how worried she was because I worried about Ethan. She told me Stuart was going to Fort Benning. When she told me Fort Benning, I wondered if it would be possible for me to send my letter with him to give to Ethan.

"In the evening, I walked to the Corners' house to talk with Stuart. I told him about the shoelace and how much I wanted to get the broken lace to Ethan. Stuart took the letter but warned me he might not ever see Ethan and he might not ever get my letter to him. I assured him I understood.

"When he shipped out two weeks later, I came to the bus station to see him off. I told him I would pray for his safety. He asked me to keep an eye on Alice. He knew she would worry about him. So I promised him I would watch after her while he was gone.

"I kept my promise. Alice and I would go for a walk every Sunday evening. We talked about how much we missed Ethan and Stuart and how we worried about their safety. It was such a comfort to have someone else to talk to who knew how I was feeling.

"About three months after Stuart left, I received a letter from Ethan. In his letter, he told me Stuart gave him my letter. He wrote that he thought about me every day, and he was eager to get back home to me so we could get married and start our life together."

"Oh, Gigi, how incredible that Stuart managed to find him and get him your letter."

"The story gets a little better," Gigi responded with a twinkle in her eye.

"Oh, please tell me!"

"Both Ethan and Stuart were wounded and sent home."

"Is that why Great-Grandpa limped?"

"Yes, he took a bullet in his leg. He came to my house the day he got home. He arrived at our front door on crutches and asked to speak to my father. Father came to the door, and Ethan immediately asked him for my hand in marriage. My father suggested we date for a while longer to make sure we belonged together. Ethan shook his head and told my father he knew we were meant to be together because I had saved his life.

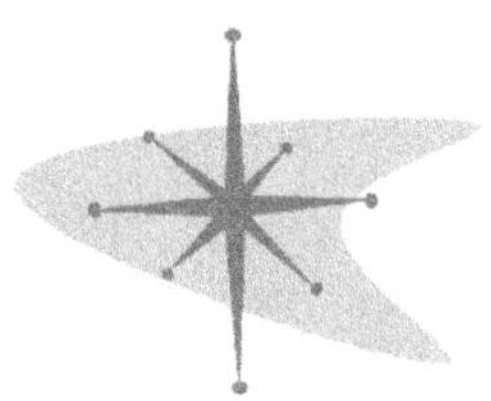

"Ethan and Stuart were in a foxhole together. The battle was not going well. Things had gotten so bad their platoon was preparing to retreat. Both he and Stuart were injured, and they knew they would be captured when everyone retreated. The Germans were advancing too fast. Ethan and Stuart figured they had to devise a way to slow the Nazis down, if for no other reason than to give the others in their platoon a chance to get away. They had one grenade left between the two of them. They knew if they waited to see the enemy until they threw it, it would be too late. So they decided to use the grenade like a stick of dynamite and have it blow up that specific section of the foxhole. If they could destroy the foxhole, they might stop the Nazi's ability to use the foxhole to advance toward the Allied forces. Ethan reached into his pocket for a coin. They were going to flip the coin to decide who would stay back with the grenade. As his hand dug into the pocket, he felt the shoelace he always kept there. He pulled it out, and both he and Stuart looked at the shoelace and realized they could use it as a timing device to delay the detonation of the grenade. They wrapped the shoelace around the safety lever. Once it was tied tight enough that it held the safety lever in place, they pulled the pin. Finally, they set the shoelace on fire and hobbled as fast as they could away from it. The shoelace gave them enough time to get safely away while destroying a segment of the foxhole. They not only saved themselves but protected their entire platoon.

"After telling his story, he looked at my father and said I had sent him the shoelace and asked him to stay safe. He told my father he knew in his heart God had let me find Stuart so he could get my letter, which had the shoelace in it, which eventually saved both their lives."

"One day, one week, or one month; one year, five years, or fifty years could pass, and I would still know in my heart that God made Irene just for me," he told my father. "I promise to love her, cherish her, and take care of her all my life."

"My father gave us his permission, and we were married four months later."

"And stayed married for the next sixty-two years," Izzy added.

"He kept his promise to my father. He loved me, cherished me, and took care of me all his days. He still provides for me even though he has been gone for ten years. I feel his love every day."

Izzy got tears in her eyes and confided in her great-grandmother, "I hope to find a love like yours someday."

"You will. Your great-grandfather and I have prayed for you to share a love like ours since the day you were born."

The thought of her grandparents praying for her to find a love like theirs warmed her heart.

After a moment, Izzy said, "But I still don't understand what's in this box?"

Gigi reached into the box and pulled out the envelope at the front.

"Your great-grandfather came home wounded very early in the war effort. The story of how my shoelace saved his life spread like wildfire. They even did a story about it for the newspaper. Other women started hearing how my "love promise," as the shoelace started being called, had saved Ethan's life, and they wanted to send their loved one a "love promise" of their own.

"Alice's cousin Dorothy was the first to come to see me. Her fiancé Joseph had been drafted, and she wanted to send him a bottle cap from a soda bottle. She told me how on every date they had, Joseph would keep the bottle cap from the cream soda bottle they shared. Then, at the end of the night, he would flip the bottle cap. If it landed with the inside of the cap facing up, he would get an extra goodnight kiss.

"Her heart was convinced. She needed to send him a bottle cap "love promise" so he would know she was thinking about him and praying for him. She said she didn't know of anyone else who had been drafted and had no idea how she was going to get her letter to Joseph. So I agreed to find a way to get Joseph's letter to him."

"Gigi, you still have the letter."

"I tried to find someone who had been sent to Fort Chaffee in Arkansas, but no matter what I did, I couldn't find anyone. I had no idea where he had been sent other than Fort Chaffee.

I also didn't know where he was serving. If I knew that, I would have just mailed it to him myself."

"Joseph probably doesn't need the bottle cap any longer, Gigi," Izzy gently said. "We probably could throw it out."

"I can't, Izzy. I promised Dorothy I would get her letter to Joseph, and as long as I still have the letter, I can try to fulfill my promise. If I throw away their love promise, I feel like I broke my promise. It's irrational, I know. But it still feels that way in my heart."

"So what are we going to do with this box?"

Gigi looked at her for a long moment and then asked, "Will you promise to try and help me deliver these love promises?"

"Gigi, how in the world will *I* ever be able to deliver these now! These people might be gone."

"Please, Izzy? Please help me fulfill my promise and help me deliver these letters."

Izzy looked back at the woman who meant the world to her and quietly said, "Yes, Gigi, I'll help you deliver these love promises."

Gigi and Izzy will be back in future stories in the Love Promises Collection.

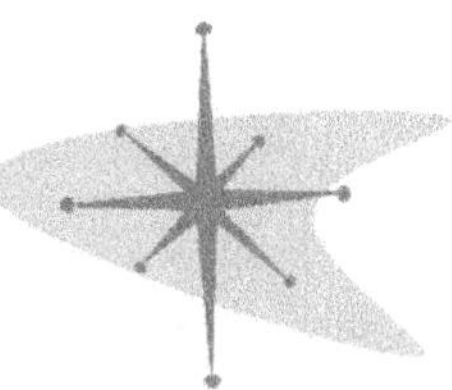

About the Author

C. Kelly, Thrown by Love's award-winning romance author, reveled in the challenge of writing this short story and looks forward to writing more stories for the Love Promises Collection. When she's not writing, she loves laughing and spending time with her family in Minnesota.

https://www.authorckelly.com

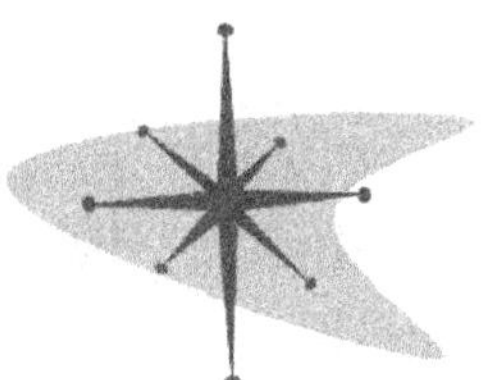

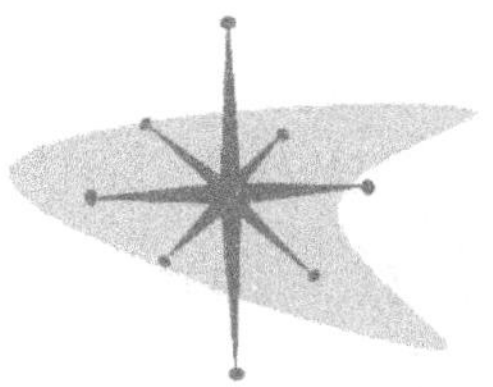

Meeting Again, 50 Years Later

by Gloria VanDemmeltraadt

Judy McKenzie was excited about going to her 50th class reunion. She had graduated along with 149 others from Deep Lake High School in the smallish town of Deep Lake, Minnesota, in 1962. The class held periodic reunions through the years, being close to the Twin Cities of Minneapolis and St. Paul, where many of the class members lived, but Judy had moved from the area when she married her husband, Matt, and this was the first reunion she was able to attend.

Judy and Matt had met in college, and because of Matt's involvement in his father's business in Pittsburgh, Pennsylvania, that's where they lived for all their marriage. They raised two daughters and a son in a comfortable suburb, and Judy was able to be a stay-at-home mom in their community. Unfortunately, Matt developed a brutal case of cancer that resisted all treatment, and he passed away at age 59.

Life as a widow was tough for Judy. She had many friends in her community, plus Matt's family, and many of them were doing all they could to help her adjust. But after losing her husband, she longed to be closer to her own children. Surprisingly, all three of her children had chosen or were led to make their homes in Minnesota because of their work or personal relationships. Her son worked for 3M and lived near St. Paul, where 3M headquarters were located. One daughter became a nurse and worked at the Mayo Clinic in Rochester, and the other was already an established dentist in the small city of Brainerd, to the north.

With help from her daughters especially, Judy found a wonderful apartment in an assisted-living building for seniors in a St. Paul suburb. She didn't need help with daily living now but was assured that if she did need help, she wouldn't have to move again to get it. Moving was the hardest thing she had ever done, and she was amazed that she survived the process. She was now determined that she would never move again, and her motto became, "Use it or pitch it," concerning her possessions. Her children, overloaded with once-precious mementos of their lives in Pennsylvania, heartily agreed.

Deep Lake was not far from Judy's home in St. Paul, and when she got her notice of the 50th reunion, she called an old friend who had stayed in touch through Christmas letters and still lived in Deep Lake. "Hey Faye, guess who has moved practically next door to you?"

"Oh, Judy, you can't fool me. God bless whoever invented display phones. Have you finally moved back to where you belong?"

"I have, and I already know it was the right thing to do."

Faye went on, "That it was, my friend, I can't wait to see you! My coffee pot is always on; can you come over right now?"

"I'm almost already on my way—I want to talk old Deep Lake and hear all the latest gossip."

Judy headed to Faye's. She knew the way, as Faye and her husband had bought Faye's parents' old house, which wasn't far from where Judy had lived with her own family when they were kids. However, as she drove further, streets and buildings she didn't recognize had popped up like mushrooms, and nothing looked the same. New housing developments had appeared, and old landmarks had disappeared. Then, somehow, after a number of wrong turns and backtracking a few times, she found her friend's house.

Hugging each other heartily, Faye and Judy giggled like they were kids. "Oh, this feels so good. I missed you and this place so much!" Judy sighed.

"That makes two of us," Faye agreed.

After several cups of coffee and non-stop remembering and catching up, they talked about the reunion and what it would involve. Faye said she had gone to a couple of the former reunions, but the 50th was really special. It was to be held at the city's country club, and a tour of the old high school was planned. The school had been purchased by a company that restored older buildings and was used as a sort of museum and meeting space. The girls could hardly wait to see it.

They remembered their old friends and the fun they had together. Slumber parties were a highlight, but not much slumber was ever had. Faye had some pictures of girls with grins and rollers in their hair and a pimple or two on their chins. They all sat on the floor wrapped in quilts and blankets, told ghost stories, and ate tons of potato chips and Ding Dongs. In the middle of the night, a bunch of them ran around outside trying to scare each other, but they were afraid to make too much noise because the man next door was their driver's ed teacher. Nobody wanted to jeopardize getting their driver's permits.

Judy mentioned their ninth-grade "Snow Ball," a winter dance, when the girls invited boys to the dance instead of the other way around. She said, "I was so nervous because it was really hard to ask a boy."

"No kidding," Faye responded, "I almost didn't go, but at the last minute, I asked Dougy Baker, and he said he'd go with me. That was hard!"

"I asked Robert Albertson, and I was terrified he would say no. But he didn't, and we actually danced a few dances. He was such a quiet boy. Whatever happened to him?"

Faye replied, "I dunno. I never saw him again after graduation. Who knows, he might show up at the reunion—this is gonna be an interesting time for sure!"

They talked about the old ice cream shop downtown where everybody went after school and the smoke shop across the street where no respectable girls ever went. Instead, a boys-only place called Tiny's caused no end of speculation for all the girls.

Judy said, "Remember when Elvis was real?"

Faye rolled her eyes, "Who doesn't? And the beginning of the Beatles, and Ann Margret, Peggy Lee, Pat Boone, Ricky Nelson, The Platters..." Both of them immediately stood up and sang, "Smoke gets in your eyes..." before collapsing in giggles.

Judy asked, "So, what will you wear to this gala?"

Faye answered, "Well, I lost my crinoline underskirt long ago, and if I wore my pedal pushers, I'd look like ten pounds of potatoes in a five-pound sack. Luckily, I bought a dress that covers some of my expanded curves. How about you?"

"I did the same thing. Mine is blue and looks okay with my hair. I'm not ready to be gray yet, so I keep it light blond."

Faye said, "The blond looks good on you—I'm not ready for gray either, but mine is a little dark. We're getting there, though." They both sighed.

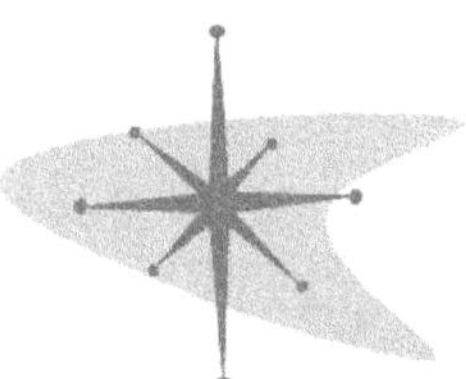

The big night arrived. Judy and Faye were lost in the middle of a large group of their high school friends, and all were hugging and squealing with joy as each new person walked in the door. Smiles and tears spread through the crowd and the sound system played all of their favorite songs throughout the evening. Some broke out dancing to the tunes, and the MC had a terrible time trying to bring some order to the gathering to make announcements.

The school tour was a highlight; some of the old classrooms had been kept as they were 50 years before. Some wooden desks even had initials carved in their tops, and the perpetrators who found them yelled their delight.

A slide show of school events played along with the music, showing cheerleaders leaping for sports events, and the sports events themselves brought major cheers and laughter. Sports heroes with heavier bellies and thinner hair shook their heads at their youthful bodies and massive muscles while wondering what happened along the way.

A large table displayed old yearbooks and photos of special events, along with some of the decorations kept by sentimental members of the class. Judy even saw a picture of herself dancing at the Snow Ball. Looking up from the photo, she suddenly locked eyes with the boy with whom she had been dancing so long ago. Robert Albertson smiled and said, "Judy. You haven't changed a minute since I held you in my arms in ninth grade and we danced to 'Mack the Knife.'"

Shocked, Judy blushed at his kind words and stuttered, "R-Robert, how nice to see you after so long."

Robert continued, "Same here. I've never come to any of the earlier reunions, but I decided this one was special, and now I see how special it is."

Now recovered, Judy replied, "I see you haven't lost your charm. It took a lot of guts for me to ask you to that dance because I wasn't dating at that time, and I didn't know you very well. You were so shy, and so was I. We had a good time, though, so I wonder why we never saw each other after that."

Robert suggested they have some punch and sit down for a real conversation. So they found a table and sat together, and Robert asked if she was there with someone.

"Not really. I came with Faye McCain tonight, but I am widowed and recently moved back to this area from out east. How about you?"

"Me, too, as a matter of fact. I was divorced many years ago, and I've always lived in New York. I'm an attorney, but I retired last year. My only daughter lives in Minneapolis, so I decided to move back here to be closer to her."

"We do have similar stories," Judy said. "I married right out of college, and we lived in Pittsburgh for many years. Then, my husband died of cancer, and I decided to move back here to be closer to my children, also."

Robert explained, "I owe you an apology for not pursuing you after that dance. I liked you very much, but you see, my parents were farmers, and I needed to work on the farm every spare moment because I was an only child. I didn't date at all in high school, as my parents not only frowned on it, but they also couldn't do without my help. I loved them dearly, and I was glad I could help them, but it wasn't enough. We struggled. Then my dad was killed in a terrible corn-picker accident, and my mother couldn't go on after that. She died herself not long after dad's accident."

"Oh, that's so sad. I'm sorry you suffered those losses."

"I survived. Not only survived but thrived after the sale of the farm and with insurance benefits. My uncles sent me to college out east, and I did well. I married a girl from college, and we had our daughter, and I joined a good firm in New York. However, the grass was always greener somewhere else for her, and my wife left me for another guy. She didn't even want her child, so I raised our daughter myself. She grew up and eventually married a guy from Minnesota, and that's how I ended up here."

Suddenly, their conversation was interrupted by other revelers, and Judy was drawn away to join a Bunny Hop that was circling the room. Robert joined the group, too, but they couldn't stay together amid the laughing, bouncing bodies.

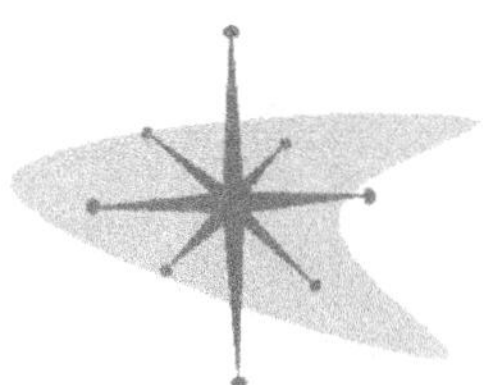

Much later, as the evening was dying down, Robert was able to catch Judy's eye, and they met again for a few minutes. Judy was intrigued by Robert and the brief glimpse she had of his life. No other man had ever caught her attention like this, and instinctively, she knew he felt the same way. In their brief time together, they exchanged phone numbers and planned to meet for coffee the next day so they could continue their conversation. Their instant mutual attraction was clear to both of them, and parting was painful.

Faye was curious about the nice-looking man Judy was chatting with and quizzed her on the way home. Judy changed the subject, and they laughed and gossiped about all their friends and the fun they had. Judy wanted to keep the interaction with Robert to herself for a while because she didn't know where it might lead. The possibilities were whirling in her mind.

Later at home, Judy said to herself, "Yes, this *was* a special reunion," as she fell asleep. *Who knows what might happen now*, she thought before dreaming of dancing in the arms of a sweet and kind young teenager with snowflakes all around them.

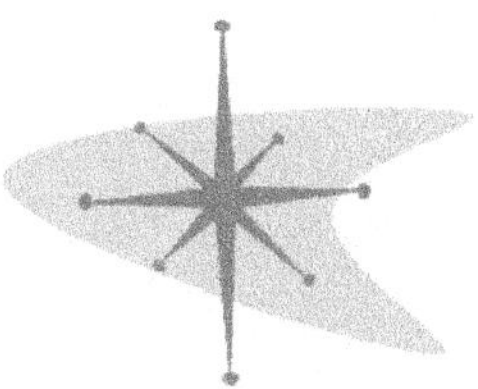

About the Author

Gloria VanDemmeltraadt
Much of her work focuses on drawing out precious memories. As a hospice volunteer, she continues to hone her gift for capturing life stories and has documented the lives of dozens of patients. She refined this gift in *Memories of Lake Elmo*, a collection of remembrances telling the evolving story of a charming village. She continues her passion and has caught the essence of her husband's early life in war-torn Indonesia. In *Darkness in Paradise*, Onno VanDemmeltraadt's story is touchingly told amid the horrors of WWII. This work has been praised by Tom Brokaw and has also earned the New Apple Award for Excellence in Independent Publishing for 2017 as the Solo Medalist for Historical Nonfiction.

The theme of legacy writing continues with a nonfiction booklet, a clear and concise how-to manual called *Capturing Your Story: Writing a Memoir Step by Step*. Gloria lives and writes in mid-Minnesota. Contact her through her website: gloriavan.com.

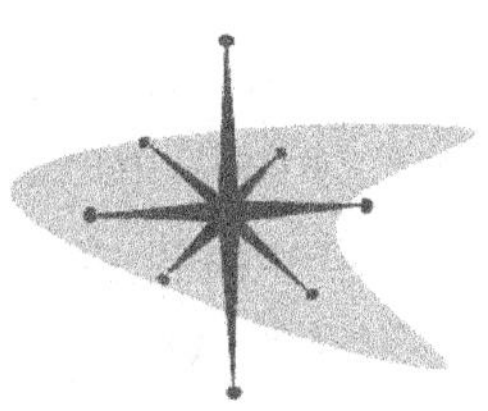

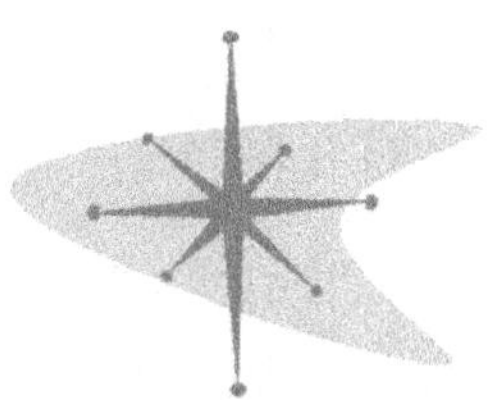

THE SECOND TIME AROUND

By **Gloria VanDemmeltraadt**

"**M**om, you are too young to be alone for the rest of your life. Dad's been gone for five years now, and to be brutally honest, you are not looking good."

"What do you mean, not looking good? I take care of myself. I do my job well and watch my weight. What are you talking about?"

"I mean, you're looking lonely. It's hard to describe, but sadness is taking over, and Jim and I think you should find someone to spend your life with. Lonely isn't your style."

I sighed. "So, how do I do that? Eligible men don't grow on trees, you know. I wouldn't have the first clue on how to date. *Date*. Egad, I haven't dated in thirty years!"

The lunch meeting with my daughter was not going well. I was hoping she might help me find some charity work or the right places to volunteer to fill my empty evenings now that she was married and had moved 50 miles from me. Her brother, Jim, recently graduated from college and had a great job offer three states away. They believed I needed to find someone to share my life with, but the very thought terrified me.

By the time lunch was over and I was sitting in my car, stunned, I realized that I had agreed to talk with my coworkers at the office where I worked as a secretary and tell them I was looking for a man. I had also agreed to change my name. I had always liked Mary Ellen, as my parents called me, but my daughter thought the name was old-fashioned and I should change it to just Mary Banks. Simple and feminine, but less grandma-sounding. After all, I was only 53 years old, and it was 1969, after all. All I could think was, "What have I got myself into?"

The worst part was that Sandy was coming back to go shopping with me to update my wardrobe. Thinking of the short skirts the younger girls in the office were wearing gave me a headache. Surely she wouldn't make me get clothes like that!

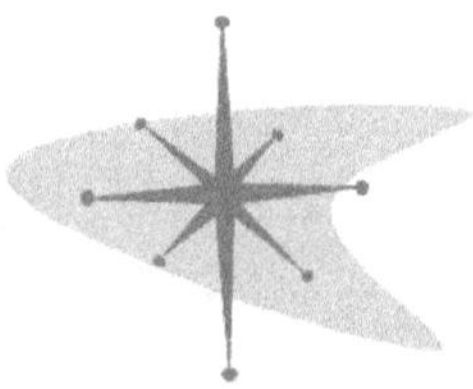

One month later

I was exhausted. Between Sandy and Jim and my coworkers, I had received a dozen telephone calls from various men. All of them wanted to know what I looked like and whether was I 'chubby' or had gray hair. They asked me to have drinks, told me about their ex-wives, mostly still living, their annoying children, and more. To a man, they bored me to tears. I couldn't do this! Better said, I didn't want to do this!

I made a date with a man who sounded nice on the phone. We met for coffee in a neutral place. It was awful. I must say he was complimentary about how I looked, but that was it. He bad mouthed his ex-wife, gave me an exhaustive list of things he didn't like and wouldn't tolerate, and said he didn't do other people's children.

That was the only one I'd dated—so far, even though I was now the owner of an updated wardrobe of fairly tasteful clothes that I had to admit looked a lot better than my old favorites. I had a new hairstyle based on the Audrey Hepburn French twist, and I was still able to pull out the few gray hairs I found. Sandy said I didn't need to color my hair yet—hair color, heaven forbid! My pastor even commented that he had heard I was looking for a husband and said he could help. I just wanted to yell, "Stop!"

Since my husband died and our children left home, I missed cooking for them. I used to enjoy cooking for company, too and making special dishes. So one day, I went to a fancier grocery store than I usually shopped, looking for something fun to cook a special dinner for myself. It was a Saturday, and I wandered around the unfamiliar store, enjoying the smells and sights of a new place. This one had a great bakery, and it smelled divine.

I was just standing there with my eyes shut and enjoying the scents when *bang*, another cart ran into mine. My eyes popped open in surprise, and I stared into another startled pair. They happened to be the bluest eyes I had ever seen and were topped by a full head of soft white hair. The man and I looked at each other in embarrassed silence for longer than comfort allowed. We then spoke at the same time and got even more embarrassed. We each laughed and then spoke again at the same time. After more laughter, he held up his hand and said, "Me first? Please accept my apology for running into you just now. I'm so sorry, but I just wasn't looking for a moment. The incredible smells coming from the bakery seemed to have me in a spell, and I just had to enjoy them with my eyes shut. Unfortunately, I kept moving with my cart."

I had to reply, "Would you believe me if I told you I was doing exactly the same thing? I was just standing here enjoying myself."

"Well, I'm sorry I hit you, but it was a pleasant moment for both of us."

"Yes, it was." Reluctantly it seemed, we moved off to do our own shopping. However, I was still a little stunned by the encounter. Not only were his eyes blue, they were kind, with smile lines around them. I felt silly thinking about the eyes of a stranger, but they stuck in my mind.

Later, as I approached the checkout counter, I saw the man again. In fact, he was right behind me in line. We both felt a little familiar now and began to chat. Finally, he said, "I suppose you're fixing dinner for your family this evening."

"No, it's only for me. My husband is gone, and my children live away now. I just wanted a nice dinner for myself. How about you?"

"It's only for me, too. I'm not married, and my kids are on their own."

Silence.

He went on. "I know this is forward of me, but the old saying is 'nothing ventured, nothing gained.' It's still morning, and it's bright outside, and I don't feel like much of a stranger anymore. Could I interest you in a cup of coffee at the little cafeteria just down the street? I'd like to continue our conversation, and I'm hoping you might be of the same mind."

"Well, it is a little forward, and my own actions are surprising me, but I'm thinking that I'd really like a cup of coffee, and someone new to talk with would be great."

We both smiled and said at the same time, "Meet you there?" followed by more laughter.

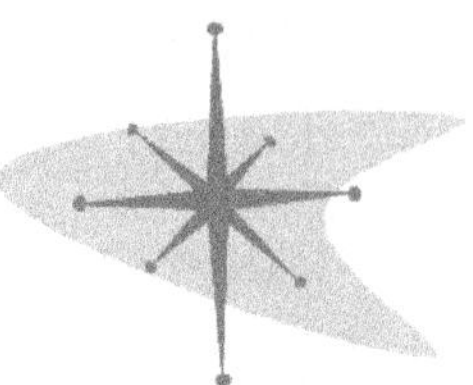

Coffee

We arrived at the cafeteria about the same time and stood outside for a minute. On entering, he said, "I guess it's time I formally introduced myself. I'm Jack Mueller, and I'm glad to meet you."

"Mary Ellen Banks. That means we aren't strangers anymore," and we walked in.

We sat down and ordered coffee and looked at each other. Then, after a moment, Jack opened with, "I don't know about you, but I can say that I never picked up anyone before from the grocery store."

"First time for me, too," and that broke the ice. We shared similar experiences about losing a spouse to death and how hard it was. We both had some funny stories to tell about when we first thought about finding someone else. In fact, we chatted freely for most of the afternoon. We had more coffee and then lunch and topped it off with dessert. He was a pharmacist, and I'm a secretary in a medical clinic, so we even had some funny stories about our work. I don't know when I had a better time with anyone.

We traded phone numbers as we left, again with reluctance, and Jack said, "Let's let a couple of days go by and think about each other. Then, may I call you?"

"You may. I've enjoyed this time together very much."

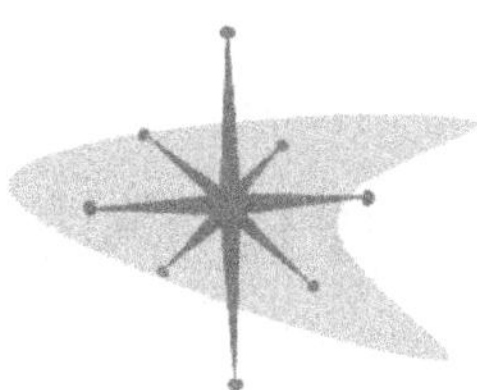

Later

Wow. I liked the part about thinking about each other for a couple of days. Finding each other was so strange and sudden and unexpected. I looked him up in the telephone book and drove by his house, that was very nice and located on the other side of town from me. I also found the pharmacy where he worked, but I didn't have the courage to go in.

At the point where I began to wonder if this amazing meeting had actually happened, Jack called. His first words were, "I was beginning to think our whole encounter was a dream, but there you are."

There I was, indeed, and our phone call lasted an hour. By the end, we had set a date for dinner for the next evening, and I know we both could hardly wait for whatever was to come.

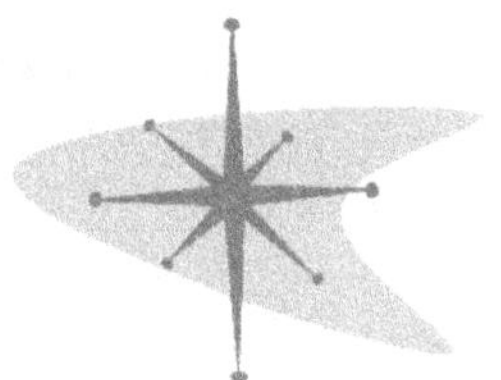

ABOUT THE AUTHOR

Gloria VanDemmeltraadt
Much of her work focuses on drawing out precious memories. As a hospice volunteer, she continues to hone her gift for capturing life stories and has documented the lives of dozens of patients. She refined this gift in *Memories of Lake Elmo*, a collection of remembrances telling the evolving story of a charming village. She continues her passion and has caught the essence of her husband's early life in war-torn Indonesia. In *Darkness in Paradise*, Onno VanDemmeltraadt's story is touchingly told amid the horrors of WWII. This work has been praised by Tom Brokaw and has also earned the New Apple Award for Excellence in Independent Publishing for 2017 as the Solo Medalist for Historical Nonfiction.

The theme of legacy writing continues with a nonfiction booklet, a clear and concise how-to manual called *Capturing Your Story: Writing a Memoir Step by Step*. Gloria lives and writes in mid-Minnesota. Contact her through her website: gloriavan.com.

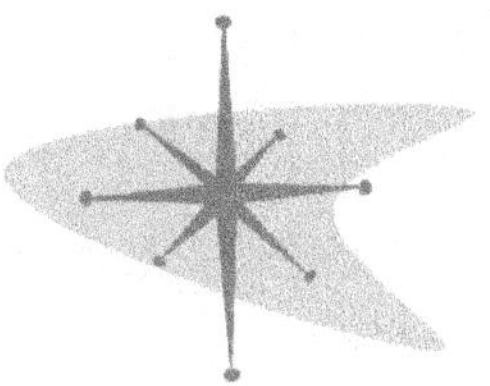

ABOUT TIME!

By Ann Aubitz

Chucky's Diner was where teenagers went to eat burgers, listen to the jukebox, and show off their hot rods. Bright and glowing inside and out, Chucky's Diner was bold and energetic, but it definitely wasn't where Mary wanted to get married.

Mary and Eddy had worked for Chucky for over ten years. Mary loved Chucky; he was her uncle. For goodness' sake, she better love him. And she loved Eddy, but Chucky's just wasn't romantic enough for a wedding.

"Come on, Mary, Chucky's will be fine. What is wrong with the diner?"

"Nothing is wrong with the diner, Eddy; I just don't want to get married here. We have worked there almost every day for ten years and got engaged there six months ago. I don't think it is necessary to do everything in our lives at Chucky's Diner. So next, you will tell me if you want us to have our children at Chucky's."

"Eww, that's just gross. People eat here!"

"I know people eat here; I'm the one that serves them their food. My point is I think we can find somewhere better to host our Christmas wedding."

Mary felt terrible raining on Eddy's parade. He was very sweet, but he just didn't have a clue about what was romantic. He actually proposed to her during a kidnapping attempt. They were at the diner when a criminal came in and ordered the meatloaf. It turned out he had stolen jewels in the next town over and was hiding out at their diner until things cooled off. Mary and Eddy were closing the diner together that night and thought the man had left. It turns out he was hiding in the back room. Luckily, Mary's brother, officer Frank, came into the diner and warned them, but there was a scuffle, and Frank was hurt. The criminal was about to take Mary when Eddy wrestled him to the ground, and Mary grabbed the gun. Right after that, Eddy proposed to Mary and told her they were the new owners of the diner.

So, of course, Mary loved the diner, but she had her heart set on getting married in the town church and having a dreamy reception somewhere else.

"Mary, I know you want a romantic venue for our wedding. Unfortunately, there just isn't one in this town. I don't want to get married in a different town; I would love to get married here."

Mary took a deep breath, "Eddy, all I said was that I wanted to check out the venue in Landsberg, that's all. I wanted to see if they have a big enough space for all our friends and family."

Eddy didn't know what to say. He wasn't very good at this stuff. He didn't think weddings were a big deal, but apparently, he was wrong. He wanted Mary's day to be special, but he just didn't know how to do that. Then, suddenly he had an idea.

"Mary, can you watch the diner for a few minutes? I need to run out and take care of something."

"Right now? In the middle of our conversation?"

"Yeah, we can pick this up where we left off. We have plenty of time to plan the wedding."

"Eddy, we are planning a Christmas wedding. Christmas is in five weeks. Some people plan their wedding for years." Mary sighed, "I swear you have marbles for brains."

Eddy grabbed his jacket from the coat rack. "I love you too! I'll be back as quickly as I can." He slid the rest of the way into his jacket when he hit the diner's front door.

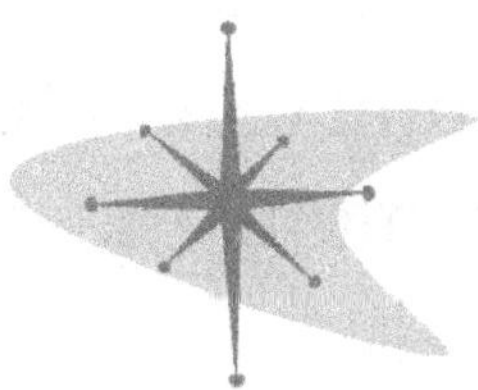

Eddy got in his brand new 1954 Chevrolet Bel-Air and started the engine. It roared to life as he fiddled with the controls. It was freezing out today, and he needed some heat, but it wasn't as cold as Mary was going to be if he didn't get this wedding thing figured out.

He really wanted to get married in the town where he was born and raised. He hadn't thought about the fact that people usually got married in the church in town and then had the reception thirty miles away in Landsberg. So he didn't think of it until Mary brought it up today.

So, he needed to figure this out for the love of his life. Eddy knew from the moment he met Mary that he would marry her. Unfortunately, the timing never worked out quite right, and they didn't get engaged until they were twenty-six years old. That was totally his fault. He chickened out so many times. Finally, he concocted a plan. He sent her notes for a week as a secret admirer to get her in the mood for the proposal. So many things went wrong with his plan that he was shocked that she even agreed to marry him.

Thinking about the wedding venue, he drove to his mom's house—Mom would know what to do. She was a good sounding board for him. She always had been. After his dad passed, she was both mom and dad to an angry little boy.

He pulled into the circular drive, admiring the Adirondack chairs on the porch all lined up for visitors—not that anyone would sit out on on a chilly November day. The squeaking sign tore his attention away from the porch and over to the old wooden sign that read "Deep Woods Tree Farm."

He vaguely remembered the day that his dad hung it. He was only six when his dad died, so memories for him were just vague recollections.

"Oh honey, why didn't you call to say that you would be coming over? I would have made some of your favorite chocolate chip cookies."

"It was a spur-of-the-moment decision. I wanted to talk to you about the wedding. But give me just a minute to get the tools out of the shed and fix your squeaking sign."

"Oh honey, that is not important right now. I would much rather have you tell me what is on your mind."

"Just give me a minute, Ma. I promise I will tell you everything when I get inside."

"Okay, be careful with that shed door; it sticks. You wouldn't want to get yourself locked in."

Eddy chuckled as his mom walked back inside the house. The funny thing was that the shed door had always stuck. He remembered when he and Mary got stuck in the shed and had to wait a couple of hours to get out. They were only eleven years old, but Eddy remembered the day like it was yesterday. That is the day he knew that she was the one for him. He knew because those two hours with her felt like two minutes. They had always had an easy camaraderie.

He trudged through the snow to get to the shed. He wanted to remind his mom to get on the tree farm employees out here to shovel a path to the house in case his mom needed it. He walked back to the house, pausing at the white gazebo—it had seen better days. The white paint was peeling in multiple places, and the roof needed a bit of repair. The benches looked like a critter had been chewing on them for years. He thought he might take a day in the spring and repair it. His mom used to sit out here for hours and watch him and his friends play in the backyard, in the area that led to one of the largest tree farms in the state.

About fifty yards in the back of the gazebo was the biggest red barn around for miles. He remembered good times, playing in the barn when he was young. The barn never housed animals of any kind but was a storage place for the Christmas trees they would sell to those who didn't want to cut their own tree down. It always smelled of a mix of fresh pine and sawdust.

He could hear people in the back talking, so customers must be there. They could come in through the back road, so they didn't pass the house. The barn looked good, but he still made a mental note to check out the barn to see if any repairs were needed. Although his mom had a large workforce for the tree lot, he still helped as much as possible. Many people assumed he would take over the tree lot when he was old enough, but he always loved the diner, and even more now that he and the love of his life ran it together.

He fixed the sign, returned the tools to the shed, and then walked back to the house's front door. He could go to the back door but didn't want to make another path with his boots. So instead, he thought he would use the one he had already made. Inside the house, he removed his snowy boots and hugged his mom.

"Thank you for being here."

"I am always here for you, Eddy. Let's sit at the kitchen table so you can tell me what's wrong."

They walked down the hallway into the spacious kitchen. Eddy's mom wanted a large kitchen, so he helped her put it in a few years ago. He didn't really know what he was doing, but he was patient, and several of his and his buddy's dads helped him.

Once seated, she turned to him and asked, "Now, Eddy, what is troubling you?"

"It's the wedding, Mom."

"What about the wedding? Do you have cold feet?"

"No, of course not. I have known Mary would be my wife since we were twelve and locked in the shed for two hours."

His mom laughed, "Oh, Eddy dear, it wasn't two hours; it was about twenty minutes."

"Well, at the time, it seemed like three hours. I learned so much about Mary."

"So, what is the issue with the wedding if it's not cold feet?"

"I was really hoping that we could get married at St. Peter's in town, then have the reception at the diner."

Eddy's mom tried to hide her smile. "And let me guess, that didn't go over well."

"No, it didn't. How did you guess?"

"You both spend all your time at the diner. I can't imagine that she would want to get married there. It isn't special enough."

"I think the diner is pretty special."

"I didn't mean it like that. I just meant that it's not special enough for a wedding."

"That's what Mary said."

"So, where does she want to have the wedding?"

"She wants to get married at the church in town, then go to Landsberg and have it at the town hall."

"Well, it makes sense. That is what most folks do around here."

"That's what Mary said too."

"Well, she is a pretty smart woman. I take that back, she is a brilliant woman because she is in love with you."

"Aww, thanks, Mom."

Eddy stood up and walked around the table to give a big hug to his mom. He knew that she was the one to help him through this.

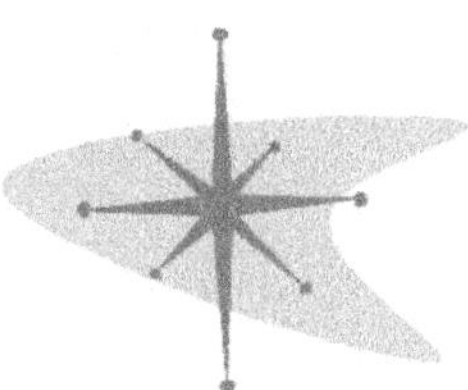

Eddy and Mary toured the town hall in Landsberg the next day and signed the contract for December 24, 1954, Christmas Eve.

"Thank you, Eddy," Mary said as they walked out of the venue. Eddy opened the door ahead of her and winced as the wind came up and whipped his face with an icy blast. Then, he turned to face her.

"For what?"

"Thank you for coming with me today and signing the paperwork for the venue. I know this isn't exactly what you wanted."

"It's okay, Mary. I know we don't have a ton of options in Sunnydale. I just wanted it to be closer to home, but it doesn't matter where we get married or where we have the reception. All that matters is that I am marrying you."

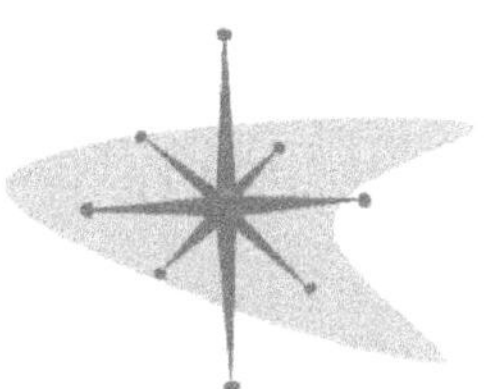

Two weeks before the wedding...

"You have a what?"

"A burst pipe," Mr. Anderson, the manager of the town hall in Landsberg, said. "I am sorry, but that means we will not be able to host your Christmas Eve wedding reception."

"You what?"

"I am sorry, Eddy, but we have no other course of action. We have to shut down. There is too much damage for us to have anything at our venue until the damage is fixed. They are saying it could be months until that happens."

"But I don't want to wait months to get married, and your venue is the only one within a sixty-mile radius of Sunnydale."

"Again, I am terribly sorry, but I don't know what else to say. I will give you first choice of any date once we are up and running, and I will throw in a discount."

"Thank you, Mr. Anderson, I know it is not your fault, and you are doing everything you can, but I just don't want to disappoint Mary."

"I know how you feel, son. I have been married for thirty years. I would do anything not to disappoint my Denise. How about you talk it over with Mary and let me know what she thinks."

Eddy knew exactly what Mary would think. She would be so disappointed that she couldn't have her Christmas Eve wedding.

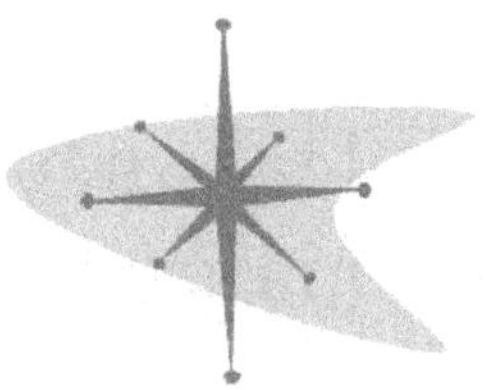

"I don't know what to do, Mom."

Eddy was sitting at her kitchen table talking about the burst pipe. He hadn't told Mary yet because he wanted to get his mom's take on the situation.

"Oh, Eddy, I am so sorry." She grasped his hand. "I promise you we will figure out something."

"Thanks, Mom." The kitchen table was in front of the big picture window that overlooked the backyard. Where the Gazebo, shed, and the barn was located. Eddy's dad built it this way so he could see what was going on even when he wasn't at work. His mom loved the gazebo view, which was also one of Mary's favorite places on the tree farm.

"That's it!"

"What's it, son?"

"The gazebo."

"What about the gazebo?"

"We can get married there. It is one of Mary's favorite places in the whole world. We can get married in the gazebo with our guests surrounding us and have the reception in the barn."

"Whoa, Eddy, that will take a ton of work, and we only have two weeks. Why don't you discuss it with Mary and see what she thinks?"

"I don't think I want to talk to her about it because I don't want her to think that we have to wait until the facility in Landsberg is fixed. I waited so long to propose that I just want to get married as soon as possible."

"I understand, honey, but to have an event of this magnitude in such a short time may not be possible."

"I can do it, mom, with help from our friends and family."

"Yes, you definitely would need help. And I will do everything I can to make this happen for you. So what's our first task?"

"I need you to call everyone and tell them the location has changed. Please let them know not to tell Mary. I will call her family and the pastor and tell them what is happening. I bet they would be able to help too!"

"Okay, son, I will start calling."

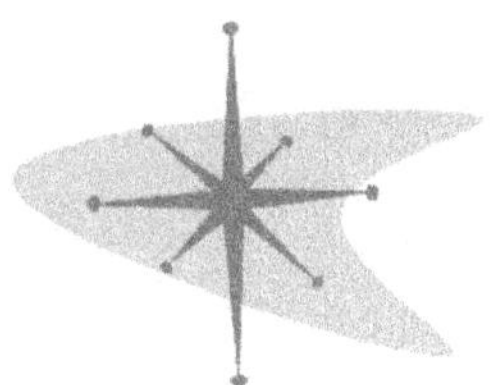

Eddy and his mom worked up a schedule and had the place look beautiful within two weeks. Almost everyone in town helped, and miraculously Mary never found out. She knew something was happening, but she figured it was Eddy being Eddy.

Eddy bought up every poinsettia he could find and made the gazebo a beautiful Christmas fairy tale for his new bride.

On the afternoon of December twenty-third, he walked into the diner and brought some fresh snow in with him.

"Eddy, how much snow are you bringing in? I don't want to have to mop again."

"Let's close up."

"What? Why?"

"Because I want to show you something."

"Is it what you have been working on for the last two weeks?"

"You knew I was working on something?"

"Yes, Eddy, you are not very sneaky."

"Well, okay, smarty pants, are you ready to see what it is?"

"Right now?"

"Yes, right now. And you have to put this on too." Eddy held a beautiful pink silk scarf in his hand.

"Seriously, Eddy?"

"Yes, please, Mary, just go along with it. I know you will love it."

Mary grabbed the scarf from his hands and put it around her head to cover her eyes. Eddy grabbed her coat and gently led her out the door and to his car.

"So help me, Eddy, if you let me fall, you will never hear the end of it as long as I live."

"I won't let you fall. I promise."

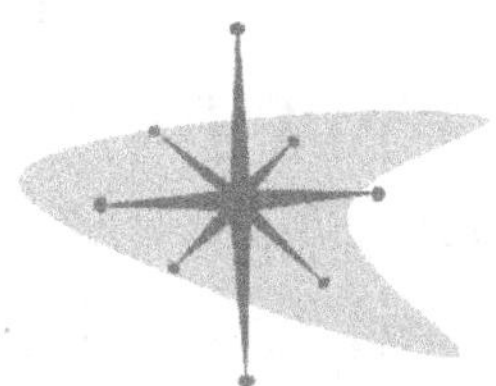

He drove the distance to his mother's tree farm. The whole way, Mary was grilling him about where they were going. She made a million guesses, but of course, none were correct. Finally, they were there.

"Okay, Mary, I will guide you out. Please keep your blindfold in place until I tell you to take it off."

Eddy was proud of himself—the gazebo had been transformed. First, he and his friends fixed the roof and the slats that needed replacing, then he built a new bench and repainted the whole thing white. Next, he bought every poinsettia he could find in town and even had his buddy take a trip to Landsberg and buy every plant they had. Next, he put all the poinsettias around the inside of the gazebo so the beautiful red flowers would surround them as they were married. Then he hung large white bulbs on the outside rim of the gazebo and barn and lined the roof with them, too—it looked magical.

"Alright, we are here."

"Now, will you tell me what you have been up to?"

"I changed the location of our wedding."

"You what?" She ripped her blindfold off and faced him. "Why?" she asked him without looking around.

"Mr. Anderson from the venue in Landsberg called me about two weeks ago and said they had a burst pipe, so we couldn't have our reception there until it was fixed, which could be months. I didn't want to wait, so I, well we, created this." Eddy swept his arms out toward the gazebo and the barn.

Mary gasped, brought her hands to her face, and started to weep.

"Now that I say all this out loud, I guess I should have told you, but I wanted to surprise you and show you how much you are loved. Not just by me, but our whole family." As Eddy said this, their family and friends poured out of the barn. "Mary, please say something."

"Ed-dy." She was crying and hiccuping at the same time. "Ed-dy."

"I know I have marbles for brains."

Mary stopped crying, took his hands in hers, and took a deep breath to steady herself.

"No, I was going to say, Eddy, you are an amazing man, and I am so grateful to marry you tomorrow and become your wife." Tears were streaming down her face.

Eddy looked surprised for a minute, then he took her face in his hands and planted a big kiss on her lips.

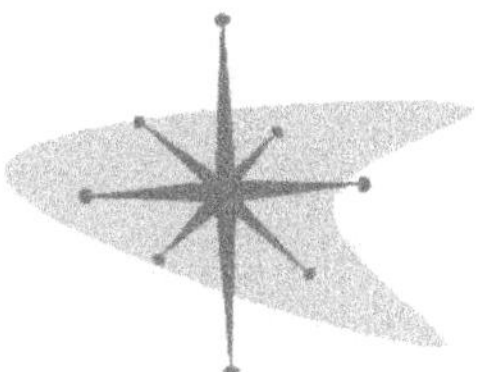

The next day, Christmas Eve, 1954, Eddy and Mary were married in the gazebo, surrounded by their friends and family.

The pastor announced, "Because they had exchanged their vows before God and these witnesses pledged their commitment to the other and declared the same by joining hands and exchanging rings, I now pronounce that they are husband and wife. Eddy, you may kiss the bride."

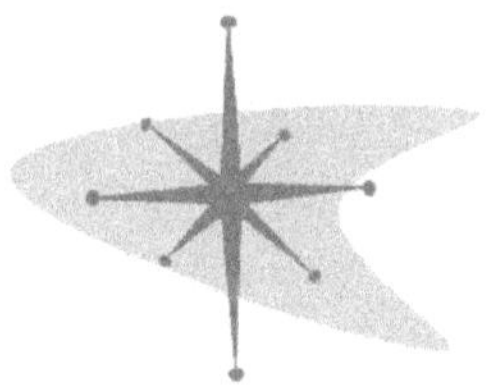

About the Author

Ann Aubitz is the co-owner and publisher of Kirk House Publishers and FuzionPress, located in Burnsville, Minnesota. After years of reading everything she could get her hands on, she decided to help others achieve their dream of becoming an author. Her mission is to help authors reach their goals by seeing their books in print.

Ann is also a proud member of the Independent Book Publishers Association, a board member-at-large for the Midwest Independent Publishers Association, and a group leader for Women of Words (WOW). She also chairs the yearly WOW writing conference.

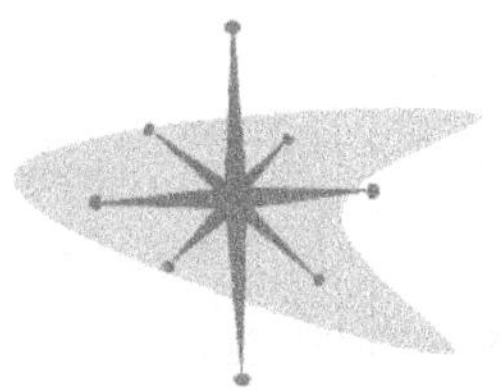

Wow, a Real Date?

By Ava Florian Johns

"**R**obert, where are we going?" Patty said rather suspiciously. The last time he took her on a date, they ended up at the bowling alley with his friends. There had been an incident with a local gang of hoodlums, and Patty had ended up saving the day by foiling their heist.

"We are going on a date, Patty," Robert said in his most confident manner. He was always confident, and people flocked to him like a moth to a flame. His mother often said that he would be mayor one day.

Patty thought, *not this again* but said, "Okay, why won't you tell me where we are going?" Inside, Patty was dreading this. She and Robert had never gone on an actual date together—or in the middle of the day.

"Because I want to surprise you. You have heard of surprises before?"

"Yes, smarty pants, I have heard of surprises, but it doesn't mean I like them."

"You'll love this one."

"If you say so, but you remember what happened last time we went on a date?"

"Yes, I remember. This time it's just us."

"You promise?"

"I promise, no hoodlums, no bowling, and none of my friends—just the two of us." Robert smiled at Patty's questioning.

"Well, about time."

"Oh, Patty, you are something else."

"I am, and don't you forget it." Patty threw her long blonde hair sassily over her shoulder as Robert chuckled.

After that exchange, they quietly rode, enjoying the sweet ride from Robert's brand new blue 1959 Cadillac Coupe de Ville. His dad owned the local car dealership and gave him a great deal on the car. Robert was a year older than Patty and had graduated the year before, so it was a partial graduation gift. Patty didn't know the first thing about cars, but Robert worked at the car dealership with his father and would one day own it.

"Can we turn on the radio and listen to some tunes."

Robert smiled, "Yes, this car has a killer radio."

The song "Venus" by Frankie Avalon poured through the speakers.

"YES! this is my favorite song." Patty clapped her hands together.

"I know it is. We heard it on the way into the bowling alley on our last date."

"Wow, it's cool that you remember that. I feel bad. I don't know your favorite song."

"It is 'Lonely Boy' by Paul Anka or that new one by Elvis, 'I Need Your Love Tonight.'"

"Hmm, I didn't know that. Are you going to tell me where we are going?"

"Not yet, Patty."

"In that case, can I ask you some questions?" She looked over at his driving to see his reaction.

"Like what kind of questions?"

"I just realized that you may know me better than I know you."

"Come on, Patty, you have known me since we were in diapers."

"I have known you that long, but I don't feel like I know you that well."

"Why do you say that?"

"Well, I didn't know your favorite color until you got this car and told me you got the blue one because it was your favorite. I also didn't know that your favorite song or that you even liked Elvis. But you know all my favorite stuff, you know that I love the song 'Venus' and that I love the french fries at the bowling alley."

Robert looked at her for a split second, not wanting to take his eyes off the road but wanting desperately to see the expression on her face. She was genuine and sincerely concerned that she didn't really know him.

"Okay, Patty, ask away."

"First off, what is your favorite food?"

"You know that one."

"I think I do. It's hot dogs. That's why you enter the hot dog eating contest at the county fair every summer."

"See, you know me better than you think you do. Now, what's your second question? Keep 'em coming."

"What's your favorite place?"

"That's easy, anywhere you are," Robert said smiling.

"Ha, ha, very funny."

"Why don't you think I'm being sincere? It's the truth."

"Well, that is about the nicest thing you have ever said to me. And you know my favorite place."

Robert hesitated for a second before answering.

"It's that state park that your parents took us to a few years ago, right?"

"Yep, that is still my favorite place. I remember the day like it was yesterday. We swam in the clearest lake I had ever seen, we built sandcastles on the beach, and we had a picnic on the big flat rock in the woods."

"I remember." He looked into her eyes for as long as he dared while still driving. Then he looked straight ahead and concentrated on the road.

There were moments of silence, which was okay with Robert. They never needed to fill the quiet space; they could just be together, which was a great feeling.

It was like that the day with her parents at the state park. He could honestly say it was one of the most memorable days of his life. Patty could have asked a girlfriend to go along, but instead, she asked him. That was the day that changed their relationship forever. She was 16, and he was 17, and it was the first time that they were together as girl and boy rather than just friends. Or at least that is how he thought about their relationship from that point on. He wanted to ask her out and be girlfriend and boyfriend, but he didn't know how to do that.

He was confident in everything else. He was on the debate team in high school and class president. His friends and others in the town listened to what he had to say and usually did what he suggested.

There was the issue on what was supposed to be his and Patty's first date when they went to the bowling alley. A gang of boys a little older than Robert came in and made a disruption so they could steal the money from the bowling alley owner's office. The owner thought it was one of Robert's friends, but it wasn't. If Robert hadn't suggested that the owner lock the doors until the police came, the bad guys would have gotten away with the money and the crime. The owner was pleased with Robert and Patty that night. Patty threw the bowling ball and distracted the thug until the police showed up.

Robert was confident in every aspect of his life except when it came to Patty. He knew he wanted to marry her, but he didn't know how she felt, and they hadn't gone on an actual date—so he was putting the cart before the horse.

"How much longer until we get there?"

"About five minutes. Do you have any more questions for me?"

"Okay, last question. Would you rather go to the beach or the mountains?"

"The beach, for sure."

"Hmmm, me too."

"I know."

"See, you know more about me than I know about you."

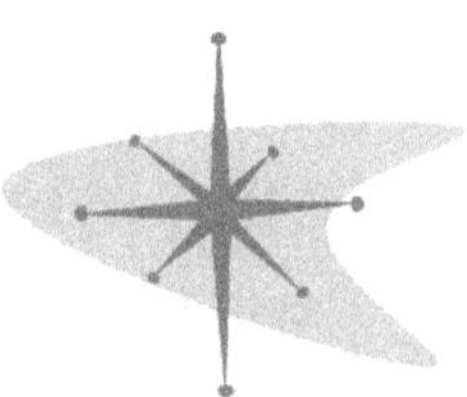

After a few more minutes of driving, Robert pulled into the parking area of a state park.

His friends were coming down the hill and to the lot.

Patty didn't realize where they were. She just saw his friends and started yelling at Robert. They were still sitting in the front seat of his car so people could see them as they walked by to get to their vehicles.

"You couldn't go one day without seeing your friends, could you? You promised me this would be different! Take me home right now!" Patty screeched at Robert. He had never heard her get so mad at him. Sure she was occasionally disappointed in him, but she had never raised her voice to him before. He was not sure what to do. Luckily his friends came to his rescue.

Freddie, Robert's best friend, went to the side of the car where Patty was sitting. "Patty, please roll down your window for a minute. I have something to say to you."

"No, Freddie, I don't want to hear what you have to say. I want Robert to take me home right this instance."

"Fine, I will talk to you through the window." Patty huffed and rolled her window down. "That's better. Patty, did you see where you are?" Patty turned red as she looked from side to side.

"Um, no, I just saw you guys, got mad, and didn't bother looking around."

She covered her head with her hands and started weeping.

"Oh Patty, honey, please don't cry. It's okay." Robert said as he rubbed her shoulder."

Patty sniffed, "You brought me to my favorite place. The place that my parents brought us that day, where we swam, played on the beach, and had that picnic on the rock."

"That's what we are doing here, and we would have been gone already, but I left my jacket by your picnic spot. Sorry to ruin the surprise. We were trying to help Robert." Freddie looked embarrassed.

"I understand, and thank you. I love it."

"But you haven't even seen it yet," Freddie asked, looking confused.

"It doesn't matter. Anywhere Robert and I are together is my new favorite place."

As they walked away, his friends all said "aww" and made kissy faces.

Patty started getting out of the car.

"Just one more minute, Patty. Now I have a question for you. Will you go steady with me?"

She answered with a kiss.

About the Author

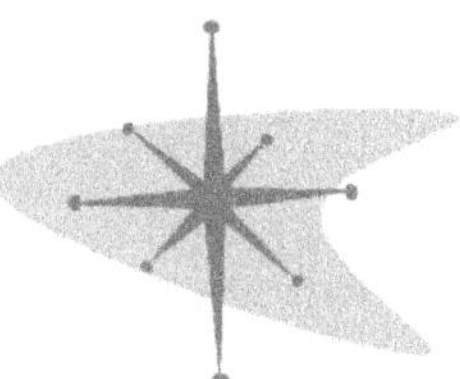

Ava Florian Johns writes in the science fiction genre. Her characters are clever and fearless, but in real life, Ava is afraid of her basement, bees, and especially clowns. Truth be told, Ava wouldn't last five minutes in one of her books.

Ava is best known for her Omega Team series.

Conclusion

Thank you for reading *Reminisce Romance*. We hope you enjoyed the stories.

Watch for the next books in our the Reminisce series to be released. They will be announced on our website. www.kirkhousepublishers.com

Reminisce Ghost Stories—Book Three

www.ingramcontent.com/pod-product-compliance
Lightning Source LLC
Chambersburg PA
CBHW080922190726
48293CB00010B/2657